The House on Plymouth Street

AND OTHER STORIES

by Ursula Curtiss

DODD, MEAD & COMPANY

NEW YORK

Many of the stories in this volume were first published in *Ellery Queen's Mystery Magazine*; "Tiger by the Tail" was first published in the *Toronto Star*; "The House on Plymouth Street" in *Cosmopolitan*, and "Snowball" in the anthology *The Lethal Sex*, edited by the Mystery Writers of America.

Published by Dodd, Mead & Company, Inc.
79 Madison Avenue, New York, N. Y. 10016
Distributed in Canada by
McClelland and Stewart Limited, Toronto
Manufactured in the United States of America
Designed by Helen Winfield
FIRST EDITION

Library of Congress Cataloging in Publication Data

Curtiss, Ursula Reilly.
The house on Plymouth Street and other stories.

1. Detective and mystery stories, American. I. Title.
PS3505.U915H6 1985   813'.54   85-1597
ISBN 0-396-08685-3

Contents

Introduction

In writing a brief introduction to my sister Ursula, as well as to this collection of her work, I shall make no comment on her books and stories. They speak, whisper, and sing for themselves.

She was born in 1923, and along with her birth certificate there was a promising heritage for a writer. Her maternal grandfather, Dr. James Michael Kieran, was a professor of English and later president of Hunter College in New York.

Her mother, Helen Kieran Reilly, was the author of over forty books, which were then generally known under the label "detective stories." Her father, Paul Reilly, was a well-known cartoonist during the twenties, published in the magazines *Judge*, *Life* (before it became a picture magazine), *Ballyhoo*, and, in England, *Punch*.

Three of her uncles, my mother's brothers, were on *The New York Times:* Leo Kieran (aviation); James Kieran (political reporting from Albany and then from the White House); and John Kieran (sports and later "Information Please").

Westport, where we grew up, was not the fashionable town it is now, but a quiet village, which was also quietly becoming an artist's colony; my mother and father, along with their friend the writer William McFee, were among the first such folk to settle there.

There were four of us, all girls, in descending order: Peggy, Mary, Ursula, and Katherine. The life we lived there as children would be almost inconceivable today. Our house was well out of town, although within walking distance (for hardy walkers, which of necessity we became).

The country occupations were climbing trees, jumping the brook or collecting white and purple violets on the willowy islands in the middle of the brook, weeding the large vegetable garden under mild protest when we wanted to earn Saturday afternoon movie money, swimming at Compo Beach, skating on a nearby pond in winter, sledding on our Flexible Flyers, and reading, reading, reading.

All the immediate above is by way of getting to why at an early age we took to writing to amuse ourselves, Ursula then about nine, I her senior by two years. We would get up very early in the morning, at sunrise, sharpen our yellow Eagle pencils in the sharpener attached to my father's drawing board, filch small sheafs of my mother's reams of yellow paper, and set to work silently scribbling at the big round scrubbed oak dining room table.

I don't think our literary efforts had any great drive, style, or theme; they were mostly the daydreams of lonely children whose way of life (and looking back I can think of worse ways) was to provide one's own, and each other's, entertainment and amusement. Once a week we would solemnly retreat to the bedroom we shared and read our stories to each other.

Of the four sisters, we two were more or less inseparable until at seventeen I went away to New York to art school. Ursula, who was remarkably good at every school subject (except algebra, which she claims I led her through by the hand) was offered college scholarships but at that time money pinched and there wasn't enough for the additional expenses. In addition, my parents were not great believers in college per se, unless in the case of preparing for specialized professions. She went to work in Westport at the Longshore Country Club, a job she enjoyed and on which she based one of her earlier books. As that was, naturally, a summer job, she next went to work on one of the two local newspapers, the *Town Crier*.

When we were in our early twenties, I (another kind of hybrid, half-artist half-writer) switched to words, finding them in every way more appealing, and got a job as copy-writer at Macy's in New York, my assigned territory being Macy's Basement. Shortly afterward, with a little maneu-vering on my part, Ursula also joined the advertising staff at Macy's. By that time I was Home Furnishings and Do-mestics and she was Fashion, mainly hats and shoes.

Macy's copy chief at the time, the gifted and delightful Margery Greenbaum, once said while we were present, "I think the Reilly girls are the laziest copywriters in New York." When asked the reason for this accusation, she said that work was apparently so burdensome to us that we wrote at record-breaking speed, just to get the job out of the way. Her burst of laughter indicated that she meant this entirely as a compliment.

Here I will tell a story which, like Ursula's own concoc-tions, was well off the beaten track, but with no sinister overtones, only great happiness. She had prepared a half-page ad for the Sunday *Times,* showing a collection of hats, the new color for which Macy's hat buyer had dreamed up: "Jersey Cream." There were perhaps ten or twelve words of her own short copy in it. Later that week my desk phone rang and a man's voice asked, "Is this Miss Reilly?" found out that it was, and went on, "I believe you wrote the hat ad headlined 'Jersey Cream'?" "No, you want my sister, Ursula Reilly, it was her ad. She wrote it." Call switched. Caller so enchanted with the ad that he arranged an interview and hired Ursula at a well-upped salary. Caller being associated with the advertising agency handling the account of a large, well-known manufacturer of fabrics, known mainly for its bedspreads. Later that year, at a company party, Ursula met the Boston sales man-ager of the fabric house. And not much later than that, she and the sales manager, John Curtiss, were married. Just on the strength of a few words: a long happy marriage and five Curtiss children.

Soon after her marriage she started writing her books, with short stories in between because she liked the flavor and speed of the form. As with many writers of mysteries, she was offered from all sides (including her cleaning woman) interesting new ways of murdering people. She once said to me in this connection, "It's not so much *who*dunit [a word she disliked] but *why* dunit," motive of course being much harder to figure out than means, especially in contemporary work, and I think Ursula's was always a look-ahead style.

Once, visiting her gynecologist when she was in the course of producing a young Curtiss, she said she couldn't get a word or question of her own in edgewise because her doctor was so eagerly supplying her with inside information on mysterious deaths.

But she ought to have been well used to this from earlier days: when she was nine or ten our family doctor came to call on some forgotten medical errand at our house. After his ministrations, my mother asked him to sit down for a cup of coffee and Ursula overheard the following exchange. "Doctor, if a man took his coffee very strong and very black would it be possible for his wife to slip arsenic into it?" "*Possible,*" cried the doctor enthusiastically, "it happens every day!"

Ursula raised her family and wrote, in a number of different places: Boston, Marblehead and Abington, Massachusetts; Santa Fe and Albuquerque, New Mexico. She has been published in England and countries all over Europe, and once beguiled her way through the Iron Curtain by having a book published in Hungary. Two of her books, first serialized, were then made into movies. *Out of the Dark* was released as *I Saw What You Did*, and *The Forbidden Garden* became *Whatever Happened to Aunt Alice?* Her short stories have appeared in many anthologies; one of these collections is used as a textbook in college writing courses.

She died in October of 1984 at the age of 61. But . . . no one who has written down valuable and enjoyable words ever really says good-bye, to anyone.

MARY McMULLEN

The House
on Plymouth Street

SHE HAD found the house by herself, that cold October day in the quiet countryside south of Boston.

The two-chimneyed white clapboard house, shuttered in gray and clearly very old, had a settled air as it stood on its slight rise well back from the road under elms. Mrs. Tyrell did not have the boldness to knock on doors and ask about properties for sale . . . but here there was a tall young girl, bundled into a blue parka and raking desultorily under a bronze-gold burn of hickory tree in a corner near the road.

Mrs. Tyrell had Bonnet with her, the large Airedale of whom the current babysitter was ridiculously afraid, but not his leash. She closed the car door against his expectant whiskers and approached the girl, who leaned on the rake and watched her come.

For her age, somewhere in the midteens, she had a colorless and surprisingly dreary face. "Hello," said Mrs. Tyrell, against her will as sprightly as a dental nurse. "My husband and I are house hunting around here—Cresset seems like a very pretty town—and I wondered if by any chance you knew of a place for sale with a few acres?"

Something wrong about the eyes, as if the light blue irises had mended imperfectly after a shattering. Retarded, thought Mrs. Tyrell with the twist at the heart of any woman with two healthy, clear-gazing children. And not all that young: at least nineteen or possibly twenty.

"I'll ask my mother," said the girl, letting the rake fall into the pile of brown leaves, and began to walk toward the house before Mrs. Tyrell could demur.

Which she had intended to do, she realized bemusedly fifteen minutes later. "Oh, no, please don't bother," would have been off the tip of her tongue if there had been even a half-second to spare.

Diners occasionally bit down on a pearl along with the oyster, somebody always won the Irish Sweepstakes—and this place, with six acres that included a stretch of woods, was for sale at approximately the price the Tyrells had been prepared to pay.

The woman who introduced herself as Helen Wadsworth delivered the information with some reluctance, standing on the walk and gripping a coat about her in the biting air. "It's all been very unexpected. My husband's company transferred him out to the West Coast with practically no warning, and the house isn't quite in condition to be shown yet. If you'd like to come back later on in the week—"

Mrs. Tyrell, looking at the cold yet handsome features, almost challengingly bare of makeup and framed in dark hair with uncompromising threads of gray, was sure that this was no coy reference to unwashed lunch dishes or a day's delay in the dusting of table tops. Equally, standing so close to the front door, which had a great burst of honeysuckle beside it, she was convinced that if she drove away she would return to find that the house had been snapped up in her absence.

She said cajolingly, "Mrs. Wadsworth, I've looked at so many houses in the last couple of months that I've stopped seeing anything but the absolute basics. I'm not shopping, honestly. We know exactly what we want, so I'd only take up a few minutes of your time."

It was far more than that.

Mrs. Wadsworth opened the door, stepped aside, followed her visitor over the threshold, said after a second's hesitation, "Excuse me," and walked rapidly deeper into the house. Mrs. Tyrell, who had absorbed with delight the wide floorboards, the deep fireplace, the views through five crisply white-silled windows, listened unabashedly.

She heard sounds from a refrigerator and then the snap and rustle of a paper bag and, "Why don't you take these over to Mr. and Mrs. Hopkins? I'm sure they skip lunch if nobody reminds them."

More order than suggestion, it was acted upon at once. Mrs. Tyrell was obscurely relieved at the faint click of a door latch. Mrs. Wadsworth, coming back, said briefly, "My daughter knows I'm selling the house, of course, but not how soon. Well, this is the living room, obviously . . ."

If she had been honest about the state of the house, and almost every room was in some degree of up-heaval, Mrs. Tyrell had been equally truthful. Weeks of viewing had trained her eye to forget paint, strip off wallpaper, empty out furniture so that only the underlying space and proportions remained.

Downstairs, along with the dining room—also fire-placed—and kitchen, still warmly scented, were the master bedroom and bath and a slip of a room, which would accommodate three-month-old Damon comfortably for some time to come. Upstairs—Mrs. Tyrell deferred the attached barn for the moment; in her mind it would be of interest chiefly to Neil and perhaps five-year-old Annie—were a corner bedroom with fireplace, bath, and a very large guest room with a trestle table against one wall. A door at its back opened on a long narrow attic.

It was an accepted fact that real-estate agents preferred not to have owners on hand; in their eagerness owners were prone to such utterances as, "We just love this place, we wouldn't dream of selling if the doctor hadn't insisted on a drier climate for my wife's arthritis."

They need not, thought Mrs. Tyrell, have worried about this owner. Mrs. Wadsworth, opening doors, was as noncommittal as if judging strange territory herself. It was a surprise when she said, apparently of the trestle table, "My mother lived with us when we first came here, and raised African violets, but then she moved to Dedham."

For some reason it sounded like mischievous incising on a tombstone. They were standing on the upper landing. Mrs. Tyrell glanced curiously at the other woman, and then craned out the window at the sound of a nasal bawl.

"That's the Pattillos' calf, next door." Mrs. Wadsworth nodded at a trim red barn visible beyond trees.

"They're from New York. At one time they had pigs and turkeys, too—living off the land was the idea, I suppose, although you'd never know it to look at them."

Now a corner of the marble mouth did flick up—in amusement? Mild contempt? "Since then they've opened a gift and book shop and only raise one calf at a time and keep a few chickens. We get all our eggs there."

Back to business. "Would you like to see the barn?"

Mrs. Tyrell didn't really care about the barn—she had made up her mind even before mounting the stairs that they must have this house—but she said yes because Neil would want all the details when she called him in London. "First, though, I have our dog in the car. I ought to let him—"

"I'd much rather you didn't," said Mrs. Wadsworth, pleasant but edged. "My daughter is extremely allergic. Oh, I know, there are dogs just down the road, and in fact when Nancy feels that one of us needs punishing she goes there and exposes herself deliberately. It's days, sometimes a week or more, before she can breathe easily without pills."

It was stated without rancor or even censure, as a lived with fact of life. "I can't stop her, and I can't control stray dogs, but I do do what I can."

"I can certainly see that," said Mrs. Tyrell with a pang at the vision of the pale, joyless face. "I'll be quick, then."

The barn, its sliding door closed on a gray Ford, its only source of sunlight two small windows high up in the loft area, was extremely cold. In addition to the expectable tools and paint cans, it housed a gas-powered garden tiller and a riding lawn mower at which Mrs. Tyrell cast an ignorant but speculative eye. There was close to a half-acre of grass in front and a deep swath in back before the field, separated by dwarf fruit trees, gave way to woods.

At the rear of the barn a Dutch door ajar on a wooden ramp led down into a stable area, which Mrs. Tyrell, by now shivering, declined to investigate. Nor was there any point in her looking at the cellar. The furnace (gas, she learned) was obviously working, and she wouldn't have known what else to ask about.

As they walked back along the passage to the kitchen, Mrs. Tyrell said "that in her husband's absence abroad, and as a formality, she would like his uncle to see the house. Would tomorrow morning be convenient?"

"Certainly," said Mrs. Wadsworth. That would give her time to locate the appraisal and the builder's report, the bill of sale and maintenance contract for the new electric pump—all the cellars in older houses in this area had water in them during the spring—and any other relevant documents from their own purchase a year ago.

Her air of calm indifference worried Mrs. Tyrell. What if she were already finding this paper search a nuisance and planning to sell instead to a friend who already knew the particulars? Fingers nervous with the momentousness of the occasion, she wrote a check for $100, adding on the line provided, "Binder on 849, Plymouth Street." Mrs. Wadsworth wrote her a receipt.

A growing awareness of Bonnet's undoubted predicament in the car kept Mrs. Tyrell's further queries
to a minimum. She and Neil had already acquired
information about schools in a number of South Shore
towns, Cresset among them. She noted down the
amount of the mortgage and the bank that held it,
the taxes, and—Neil would be proud of her—the zon-
ing.

At the kitchen door, she turned for a final glance
out at the distant woods, a weave of deep gray stitched
here and there with red and yellow. She said compul-
sively, "I hope your daughter won't mind too much."

"Oh, no. Nancy is actually very fond of her stepfa-
ther. It's the idea of having to make new friends,"
said Mrs. Wadsworth in a forthright way, "but she'll
adjust."

Mrs. Tyrell walked to the car then drove away at
a slow cruise, looking for a safe place to let Bonnet
out. She passed the Pattillos' house, shingled in smoke-
colored cedar, and, farther along on the opposite side
of the road, the dogs Mrs. Wadsworth had mentioned:
a pair of Dobermans coming alertly to their haunches
in deep grass at the tentative sound of the car engine.
Presumably, they guarded a remodeling in progress
at the corner, although at the moment there was no
sign of workmen. Mrs. Tyrell, contemplating the long
watchful heads and sculptured muscles, was glad of
the chain-link fence: Annie, having grown up with
an Airedale, had an innocent trust in all dogs.

A right turn onto a road drifted with yellow leaves
presently provided a clearing at the edge of a woods
for Bonnet. Part of *their* woods, Mrs. Tyrell realized

with pleased surprise. A few minutes later, putting off an inspection of the town center because she had told the babysitter she would be back by four, she was on her way home.

Damon slept unconcernedly in his crib, fortified by a gourmet meal of formula and saltless strained squash. Annie, as rosy-gold as he was dark, knew all about her mother's quest and was full of excited questions. Stalled by, "I think so, but we'll see," she sat on the edge of a chair while the call to London was put in.

Mrs. Tyrell had done some concentrated thinking on the return trip. It was probably true that the house would still be available when Neil returned in just under two weeks. A lot of people didn't want that much space, inside or out, or automatically distrusted anything two hundred years old, or, increasingly, preferred to huddle in the elbow-reach safety of a development.

But it was equally true that any real-estate agent who got wind of what was going on would urge upon Mrs. Wadsworth some judicious painting and grounds-manicuring. An outlay of perhaps five hundred dollars would be reflected in a two-thousand-dollar increase in the asking price.

Neil, given a detailed description, agreed. They were totally at one about the kind of house and surroundings they wanted, which was why he had left countersigned checks on a joint money account.

"You really like it, don't you?"

"Oh, Neil. Remember that place in Cohasset we thought about but it was at the far end of nowhere?

It doesn't *compare* with this."

From the particular to the general—the children, the conference, the London weather. The barman at the Little Mayfair remembered Mrs. Tyrell from a trip made when Annie was three and had asked about her. Then: "Have Charlie take a look at the house before you sign, will you?"

"I was going to. Say hello to Annie, she's sitting here like an image, and I'll call and let you know."

Charlie Tyrell was Neil's uncle, blithely retired at sixty from a number of successful careers, including one as builder. He would know all about the points of stress in an old house, septic tanks, and other exotica. Reached at seven o'clock that evening, he said that he would be delighted to drive down to Cresset the next morning but that he had an unbreakable appointment in Boston at one, so what about taking two cars?

In the morning, Annie pleaded to go along. She was an extraordinarily good and companionable child, but even the best of five-year-olds could grow difficult with fatigue, and Mrs. Tyrell promised to bring back a picture instead. "It's just going to be long business talks and there wouldn't be anything for you to do. Besides, you have to be here to see that Bonnet is very polite to Miss Coates."

Both of these arguments had validity. Under them was something of which Mrs. Tyrell was so ashamed that she covered it up swiftly, even to herself.

She was not surprised to see Charlie's rakish dark green Jaguar there ahead of her on Plymouth Street; it was his habit to drive as though headed for the next pit stop. She had braced herself for a feeling of letdown, even of severe doubt, at this second view of the house. Instead she took in with appreciation and the pride of near-ownership details that hadn't registered exactly before: the separate front door, which opened directly onto the stairs, the black banding of the white chimneys—to keep out witches, according to one New England legend.

Nancy let her in. The hair concealed by the parka's hood the day before was in thick glossy dark braids, wiping away two or three years, and her rather heavy face shone so from soap and water that it took on a faint glow from the cherry pullover she wore with jeans.

She dropped into a chair with no accompanying invitation. "My mother said to tell you they're down in the cellar."

"I'd only get in the way," said Mrs. Tyrell, compromising on an arm of the couch, "so I think I'll wait here if you don't mind."

The starred gaze riveted itself upon her with open curiosity. "Did you bring your dog?"

"No, he isn't really that fond of the car." It was a lie, which would have made Bonnet grieve into his whiskers.

Feet could be heard below, crunching on cement and then mounting the stairs, which led up to the door in the dining room. Nancy frowned at the rug as if, having used up her two utterances in prodigal fashion, she did not know what to do next. Her brow cleared with relief. She said, firm and confiding, "I'll like California."

"I'm sure you will." Again Mrs. Tyrell felt a wrench of compassion; this had been dinned into the girl like letters of the alphabet. "I've only been to San Francisco, but it's a beautiful—"

The cellar door had opened, and now Mrs. Wadsworth and Neil's uncle were in the room with greetings. "Sound as a nut," remarked Charlie of the house's underpinnings. Lean and weathered, with a debonair little gray mustache, he looked like a man who enjoyed life. The glance he shot at Mrs. Tyrell said that although professional caution was going to keep him from any real encomiums he approved wholeheartedly of the venture.

"Nancy dear—" Mrs. Wadsworth was almost unrecognizable from yesterday afternoon in a dark wool dress with a strand of pearls, her chiseled lips the palest of rose "—have you picked up your room? Mr. Tyrell has seen all of the downstairs and the barn, but I'm sure he'll want . . ."

"No housework necessary," said Charlie, smiling at Nancy—too late; obediently on her feet, she headed for the door of what would be Damon's abode and disappeared.

"Now—" With a gesture at the couch that included both her visitors, Mrs. Wadsworth sat down in a chair beside a low table and picked up papers and a bankbook. Her left hand wore a diamond like a diminished ice cube. "I talked to my husband last night, and he said that although there'll have to be a title search these would serve as proof of ownership . . ."

The business discussion that Mrs. Tyrell had described that morning to Annie had begun. The terminology now falling on the air was enough to damp any real excitement, but the wheels were in motion, and she was grateful for Charlie's expertise.

She emerged from a semidaydream about living-room curtains to discover Charlie looking purpose-fully at his watch. It was the time of late morning when he liked someone to approach him with a Bloody Mary, and Mrs. Tyrell herself would have accepted one with alacrity, but any such offer here was unlikely as the sudden appearance of a marching band.

Instead of suggesting any adjournment, however, Charlie asked if he could use the telephone and came back with an air of almost hand-rubbing enjoyment that could only have sprung from the deferral of his unbreakable appointment. If he hurried his explora-tion of the upstairs, he said, and if Mrs. Wadsworth thought he could be of any help, there would be time for him to go with her to the title company.

Mrs. Tyrell had a sensation of being picked up and swept along, but delightfully so. Although he was fond of his nephew and by extension his nephew's wife, Charles Haywood Tyrell, widower for a dozen years, was not a man to discommode himself except in what he considered to be an extremely good cause.

It was a bare twenty-five minutes later that, having handed Mrs. Wadsworth out of the Jaguar in front of the title company office—it was his plan to proceed directly to Boston from there, leaving Mrs. Tyrell to do the chauffeuring back to Plymouth Street—he said kindly, "I have all the figures you gave me, and you don't sign anything until the closing. Look around, why don't you, and meet us here in half an hour?"

Cresset was not the kind of town in which all business was conducted behind Colonial fronts, but its tree-lined residential side streets opened up cleanly on a long and curving main street whose sidewalks would also be shaded in summer. In Mrs. Tyrell's immediate radius were a flower shop, a grocery-plus-liquor store, a pair of discreetly curtained windows, which said Dressmaking on one side and Alterations on the other—and, just beyond those, two wooden signs, creaking in the wind and separated by a single entrance. Books. Gifts.

The Pattillos, the ex-New Yorkers who would be their neighbors. Mrs. Tyrell opened the door and went in.

It was a deep, pleasant place, ivory-walled, divided for three-quarters of its length by Wedgwood blue lattice work supporting occasional vines and hung at intervals with odd items: a saucy black Raggedy Ann, a bath sheet with hearts and flowers around an embroidered "Ours," a webbed golden bag holding the sparkle of two champagne glasses.

There were customers on both sides. Mrs. Tyrell devoted herself to a revolving stand of earrings in the gift area and bided her time.

A few feet away, a large woman in a toggle coat was debating over a pair of crystal salt and pepper shakers.

"They're awfully small."

"They are delicate, aren't they?"

The second speaker was presumably Mrs. Pattillo,

small and lithe in what were probably designer jeans, well-faded, with a turtlenecked burgundy top. Her short bell of hair was like mushroom silk, her makeup frankly and entertainingly just a brush of silver on her eyelids, lashes like tiny black whisk brooms, lipstick the color of rose wine.

The toggle-coated woman made her purchase. Mrs. Tyrell turned with a pair of dangling glass triangles. She said, "I'd like these, if I may," and introduced herself. "We're buying the Wadsworth house, and I thought it would be nice to come in and meet you."

Mrs. Pattillo's eyebrows flew up. "Really? Let me call Donald, he'll be thrilled. I'm Tracy, by the way, like twenty-three million other females born that year. Donald? Come over here a sec."

The man who sauntered around the end of the lattice work was tall but as supple as his wife, with fiery dark eyes and a short, immaculately clipped black beard. He said when he had welcomed Mrs. Tyrell, "Well, that was fast. We didn't even know anyone was looking at the house."

Mrs. Tyrell explained the unlikely dovetailing of circumstances. "It's expediting matters that Mrs. Wadsworth is anxious to join her husband out on the Coast."

Neither of the Pattillos turned a head or even a hair, but something passed alertly between them. The customer, patchily visible on the bookshop side, uttered the kind of cough that spoke of patience wearing thin, and Pattillo excused himself. Mrs. Tyrell paid for her earrings and departed thoughtfully.

"You're in luck," said Charlie in an aside five min-

utes later. "The house is in her name, so there won't
be any delay. The closing will be the day after tomorrow, and I think you've got a gem."

Mrs. Tyrell had known it, but it was nice to have
his seasoned endorsement. Her swift and second trip
upstairs had revealed two bonus details—an extra
linen closet and the fact that the attic had a narrow
back stairway. Dormer-windowed on both sides, it
could be painted and turned to other purposes if they
decided to use the barn loft for storage instead.

Charlie sped off in his Jaguar, and Mrs. Tyrell drove
Mrs. Wadsworth back to Plymouth Street. Apart
from, "Mr. Tyrell was so kind and very helpful,"
her passenger had nothing to offer. She was clearly
not a woman of small talk; still, the car seemed to
buzz actively with silence.

The Dobermans were not quiet today. They raced
and ranged behind the chain links like a pair of powerful whips, growling with the collected menace of
thunder before erupting into sound. As if afraid they
would give a buyer pause, Mrs. Wadsworth said,
"They never do that at night. I think children poke
sticks in at them, just because the fence is there."

And then, astonishingly, "Will you come in and
have a drink? This has all been so . . . I could certainly
use one."

An explanation of the startling offer wasn't long
in coming. The house breathed emptiness at them
when Mrs. Wadsworth used her key. She asked if
Scotch would be all right and came back with two
glasses clinking lightly with ice. When she had sat
down, she said, staring with fixity through one of

the windows that overlooked the front lawn, "I didn't
talk to my husband last night. I haven't the slightest
idea where he is. He's left me."

Mrs. Tyrell, who had been geared to something
more in the way of a toast, thought transfixedly that
her Scotch was going to go down the wrong way.
She managed, "Oh?"

Mrs. Wadsworth acknowledged this choked syllable
with a certain aloofness of her own. "It isn't the kind
of thing one cares to advertise from the rooftops, but
the Pattillos will undoubtedly tell you, and I thought
you might as well hear it from the source."

She was remembering the interval at the title company. Mrs. Tyrell was irritated at the rush of warmth
to her face, as if a perfectly natural interest in neigh-
bors-to-be had suddenly turned into snooping.

"My husband is a few years younger than I am
and very attractive to women. I accused him of an
affair, perhaps wrongly—" into Mrs. Tyrell's head
flashed an image of silvery eyelids and clear-rose lips
"—and there was a quarrel. We were outside at the
time and I imagine it was highly audible next door."

Hard to imagine the composed voice raised, and
only possible to guess from the measure of rigidity
how much this was costing her. "It wasn't the first
such quarrel, naturally, but it turned out to be the
last. Even if I could manage a place like this by myself,
which I can't, I wouldn't care to stay on in Cresset."

No, thought Mrs. Tyrell; in spite of changing stan-
dards it would be intolerable for a woman like Mrs.
Wadsworth. There were a few poisoned tongues in

any town, and it was even possible that Nancy would be speculated about as a cause of dissension.

She said simply, "I'm sorry," and Mrs. Wadsworth dismissed that with a shrug and a remote smile. "The California part is true, anyway. I do have friends there." Then, with understandable brusqueness—privacy unlocked for casual inspection by a stranger—"Unless there's anything here you want, I'm going to put up a Garage Sale notice this afternoon and get rid of everything."

And, unspoken, make a fresh, stripped-bare start. Mrs. Tyrell finished her drink and rose. She said, making the allusion with a trace of awkwardness, "I'll ask my husband about the lawn mower and garden tiller. How much are you asking?"

She had started the car before she remembered the picture promised to Annie. She got out again and snapped it, inspected the Polaroid print, and then drove off.

"I think children poke sticks in at them," Mrs. Wadsworth had said of the Dobermans—but it was Nancy who was doing just that. At the sight of the recognized car she averted her face as though oblivious and dropped her prod in the same way she had let the rake fall to the ground, although Mrs. Tyrell could have sworn that she saw a flash of silver at the prod's head.

It was not an incident worth notice—unless the dogs ever got loose and had a chance at their tormentor. The very young, and Nancy certainly qualified as that whatever her chronological age, liked to provoke reaction for its own sake; there needn't be intentional cruelty involved.

Still, Mrs. Tyrell wished that she hadn't seen it.

Annie was rapt at the photographed pair of upstairs windows that would be hers. Standing in the small back garden, which in summer supported three tomato plants, a rosebush, a dwarf peach tree, and a row of hollyhocks, she gazed around her with daring. "Is it five times as big as this?"

How to explain acreage in terms a child would understand? "This would all fit in half the front lawn," said Mrs. Tyrell.

From then on it was an afternoon of telephoning. First Neil, in London. The conference was being cut short because its president had collapsed and died of a heart attack in the small hours, so that he would be home in six days. He said yes to the mower and tiller—"I don't want to spend all my weekends looking like the *Man With a Hoe*—" and, "Better call the storage place, our stuff may be at the bottom of the heap, and get hold of Bill McGinnis."

The stuff was antique furniture left to him by a great-aunt, for most of which there had been no room in this little starter house. Bill McGinnis, a colleague of Neil's, was their own would-be house buyer.

Mrs. Tyrell was far too excited to read after dinner. She watched a made-for-television suspense movie instead, and that was a mistake. Perhaps because there had been rain tapping at the cellar window, which was the camera's frequent and suggestive focus, and there was now real rain driving against the window

at one side of her bed, she came awake with a single
stark question in her mind.

What if Mrs. Wadsworth's second version of her
husband's abrupt and permanent departure had been
as false as the first, with an air of forced-out truth
simply because it had come second?

That could mean that he had never left at all. Not
. . . upright, at least.

The question, having sidled in, settled down, and
gave birth to a few ugly young.

Marital quarrels frequently ended in violence
rather than a mere walking out. A sharp signal had
passed between the Pattillos at the mention of trans-
ferral to the West Coast. Mrs. Wadsworth was a strong
woman, but even so—

There were two vehicles in the barn.

At this point, savingly, an imaginary voice said in
the portentous tones of a low-budget-film sheriff, "Fan
out, men. I want every square foot of these woods
examined for signs of recent disturbance."

Mrs. Tyrell switched on the bedside light. It was
four-thirty, and although Damon was inching toward
a more civilized hour he would soon be demanding
his bottle. She got up and put it on to heat, eager
as much for his company as for purposes of circum-
vention. Presently, his tiny hands curled with pleasure and his perfect, threadlike black eyebrows registering little flickers of which only he knew the cause,
he was sanity made absolute.

The closing went off without incident on a cold
and soaking day. For an occasion of such import it

was surprisingly brisk and brief; perhaps, thought Mrs. Tyrell, not unlike getting married at city hall. When they were all on their feet one of the spectacled men said to Mrs. Wadsworth with a glance out at the glistening street, "I'll bet this rain and cold makes you look forward to sunny California."

"Yes, I must confess it does."

"Roy likes it out there, does he?"

"Oh, very much," said Mrs. Wadsworth.

It had been agreed that she and Nancy would be out of the house by three o'clock on Sunday, leaving the second set of keys on the living-room mantel. Although it wasn't a day to linger in the open, Mrs. Tyrell held out her hand. "I won't be seeing you again, so goodbye and good luck."

"The same to you, and thank you for being—discreet." Mrs. Wadsworth hesitated a moment in spite of the rain. "If you happen to meet a couple called Hopkins, it's all right, they know, too."

Mrs. Tyrell had turned her ignition key when there was a tap on the car window: Tracy Pattillo, looking like an exotic child in yellow oilskins. "Does this mean the deed is done?"

"Yes, I'm going to start bringing things down on Sunday."

And that was the day when, even enjoined by Saturday's six o'clock news, she had forgotten to adjust her clock.

She brought the entire household with her: Annie, Damon in a bassinet, and Bonnet. It was finally the kind of day that October was supposed to bring, crisp, leaf-scented, with an occasional chase of white clouds across a sky of brilliant blue.

The barn stood open and empty. Damon was oblivious in his nest on the back seat. Leave him, for the moment; warm and fed and lulled by the trip, he was in the deepest part of his afternoon sleep. Mrs. Tyrell closed the car door gently, walked across the lawn to where Annie and the Airedale waited and used the front door key for the first time.

The living room, now furnished only with a shift of tree shadows on walls and floorboards, seemed to have grown in size. It greeted them with a warm, familiar aroma—poultry seasoning? Maybe the quarrel hadn't been about a woman at all, thought Mrs. Tyrell, giddy with ownership; maybe it had started out with, "Do you have to put that damned stuff in everything?"

And there with suddenness in the doorway to the dining room, causing a fast slam of fear in the throat because she had come so silently, was Mrs. Wadsworth.

She had undergone another of her transformations and wore trim gray slacks and an open-necked white shirt with the sleeves rolled up. "Mrs. Tyrell. I thought when I heard the car that you were Nancy. She's doing a few last-minute errands, and we'll be ready to leave as soon as she gets back." She added pointedly, "It *is* only two o'clock."

Mrs. Tyrell, her error explained to her, felt strangely stung and self-conscious. "I'm so sorry, I don't know how I did that. I've brought a few things to put in the barn, and then we'll be around outside. Please, take your time."

Mrs. Wadsworth had retreated a step into the dining room when she said with sharpness, "Your dog."

Bonnet, having completed a speedy investigation of the bedroom to the left of the hall, was advancing toward them on his tightly fleeced, pillary brown legs.

Mrs. Tyrell checked him with a hand on his collar. Two days ago, before she had seen Nancy at the fence with the cane, she would have offered to incarcerate him until the Wadsworths' departure. Now she said, "I'll see that he stays with us," and ushered them all out the door.

Bonnet rushed off at once to search for a stick; an otherwise mature six, he lost his head at the sight of any kind of running space. Damon hadn't stirred. Mrs. Tyrell opened the trunk, and between them she and Annie carried brushes, an old sheet, and cans of paint—a glowing white to replace the living room's yellowing cream—into the barn.

Annie was captivated by the echoing hollowness and the smells of earth, old wood, long-gone hay. She called from the stable area, "Did the horse live here?"

"Once, I suppose." Mrs. Tyrell walked down the ramp toward where the child had positioned herself solemnly at the back of a stall as if to get a horse's-eye view of things. "We have to go outside awhile, Annie, until the people leave."

Annie's navy coat was caught on what turned out to be a nail. Mrs. Tyrell freed her, heard the lightest of sounds from the layering of dusty straw, and put a hand to her ear. She had considered the glass triangles somehow appropriate for this day, and one of them had dropped off.

She was fond of the earrings, which shone with icy clarity inside the curve of her hair, once the color of Annie's but now turning darker. She moved the straw carefully and experimentally with the tip of her shoe: Glass would drink up and reflect even this filtered light.

But what she was looking at, and what gradually revealed itself to be a great stain, almost torso-sized, was blood. Not very old blood, because it was still readily identifiable as such.

The bottom half of the stable door clicked shut. "He was going to do something dreadful to my daughter," said Mrs. Wadsworth, standing behind it. There hadn't even been a warning gather of drum rolls; she was simply there. "Just because she got out of temper and tried to . . . He was going to put her away."

At the first words, the past-tense words, Mrs. Tyrell had reached for and was gripping Annie's hand; it shivered through her head like lightning that unless Mrs. Wadsworth had gone right up to the car she couldn't know Damon was there. The same flash showed her the source of the shame she hadn't wanted to examine before. Mixed with her compassion, from the first, had been a slight recoil from Nancy. Had the similarity of names troubled her? Certainly she had not wanted her child exposed to the flawed gaze, which, translated into terms of sound, would be a steady, busy drill.

Not retarded, but unbalanced and dangerous.

As if she hadn't grasped what she had been told, Mrs. Tyrell got words past a heavy, hard-beating pulse. "My husband's uncle is meeting us here. In fact, I think—is that his car?"

Mrs. Wadsworth didn't trouble to turn her head. "Nancy will be twenty-one in the spring, and then she comes into the principal of her grandmother's inheritance—such a dear little thing she was, when she was three. I couldn't have court-appointed people prying around after all these years."

The years when she had had control of the income—and the prospect of the years ahead. In consequence, the ultimate action taken, here in an old New England barn, with Mrs. Tyrell stumbling into it like a rabbit into a snare.

Her unconscious had suggested more than she knew during those rainy small hours. It presented her now with the trim red barn so readily to hand, its owners away all day, which undoubtedly contained things like cleavers, because who could cope with whole steers or pigs?

But then what had been done with Roy Wadsworth? Any extensive digging would soon betray itself in wet ground, and the Pattillos were already dubious about the transferal to the West Coast.

A remembered smell of poultry seasoning, not once but twice, mingled with a few remembered words and caught sickeningly at the back of Mrs. Tyrell's mouth. She said, taking a bold two steps closer to the stable door, "I haven't the slightest idea of what you're talking about, but whatever it is it has noth-

ing to do with me. I'd like to show Annie the back,
so—"

It had had to be tried, and of course it failed. Mrs.
Wadsworth said in an appallingly conversational
voice, "Nancy will be here any minute."

*And if Nancy comes, if there are two of them, we are
lost.*

Mrs. Tyrell measured her as she imagined men in
a fighting mood measured each other. She was out-
topped by two inches and outweighed by about
twenty pounds. And there was Annie, not quite com-
prehending but holding her hand very tightly, to
think about.

And, in the car, Damon. So very small, so—disposa-
ble. Bassinet wicker burned up in a flash.

Mrs. Tyrell moved her gaze, craning for a view
of the lawn. She saw Bonnet, beside the car and gnawing at a stick clasped between his forepaws even
though nobody had played with him. She said with
an air of vindictive triumph, "You'd better take away
that thing my dog has, before he runs out in the road
with it."

The clear fear of a dog on these premises, with
the according tale of severe allergy. How sure could
a spur-of-the-moment killer be that the tidying had
been complete?

Mrs. Wadsworth half-spun and went crashing
down against the tiller as Mrs. Tyrell, up the ramp
in less than a blink, sent the stable door flying at
her with the desperate strength of knowing that this
chance could not be achieved again.

Her chest hurt. "Annie, run and get in the car,

quick, and lock your door. No, you don't," she gasped
to Mrs. Wadsworth, struggling to rise with a beginning trickle of blood at one side of her chilly white
forehead. *"No, you don't."*

She had never in her life inflicted deliberate harm
on another human being, and even at this moment
it was difficult to get down on one knee, seize the
shirted shoulders, bang the gray-threaded dark head
against metal with a force that terrified her. Then
she was up and running across uneven planks—*dear
God, don't let me trip*—toward sunlight.

She reached the car, shaking so that she had to
wrench twice at the door, and somehow got in. With
what felt like the last of her breath she called to Bonnet who, believing that a game had finally begun,
had pounced across the lawn.

And out of the barn came Mrs. Wadsworth, lurch-
ing, horrifying, with a lawn edger grasped like a jave-
lin.

Leave Bonnet—after his years of nursemaiding Annie, his vigilant new station beside Damon's crib?
Carry away the memory of the stick sprouting hope-
fully out either side of his whiskers?

"Bonnet, come!" shrieked Mrs. Tyrell, and at the
last possible second he dropped the stick, bounded
forward, and scrambled into the car.

By the sheerest providence and because the house
had looked so empty, the keys dangled from the ignition. Mrs. Tyrell was backing without so much as a
glance over her shoulder when the lawn edger struck
the windshield with a force that would have cut flesh

to the bone. Damon woke up and gave a tiny querulous bleat, but they were out of the driveway and
safely on the road.

Annie said an awestricken, "Mama—" and Mrs. Tyrell said tensely, "Wait, Annie," because it took all
her trembling concentration to reach the corner, turn
right, pull off at the clearing beside the woods. (A
single and necessary trip made to the Wadsworth
part?)

Heart slowing somewhat, she looked at her child.
Annie said, "Was that lady crazy?"

Mrs. Tyrell considered it with care. *Sick* was the
gentler, more acceptable, clinical term, but measles
and mumps and chicken pox still lay in wait for a
five-year-old who might wake in the night and think—

"Yes," she said. Murder for gain might be almost
as prevalent as the common cold—but a private chris-
tening party, so that names could be used openly and
with wicked amusement?

She waited at the clearing, engine running no matter what it might cost in gasoline because she did
not dare take the smallest chance. Was it eight minutes
or twelve or fifteen before the gray Ford appeared,
Nancy at the wheel, and angled south?

Mrs. Tyrell memorized the license plate, but she
did not go immediately in search of a telephone. Instead, although she was now quite sure of what Nancy
had been doing with the cane, she made a last visit
to the deep grass behind the chain-link fence.

She got out of the car. She said flinchingly to the
Dobermans, side by side ten feet away, at once alert

and lazy on their forefeet, "Mr. Hopkins?" and then, "Mrs. Hopkins?"

And, eyes sharpening to a terrible expectancy, they came.

She was certain, now, how Mrs. Wadsworth had disposed of her husband's remains.

The Right Perspective

NOTHING COULD have seemed less menacing than the first of the activities which set tongues wagging in Earlsgate Crescent that June. It was merely the sight of Jason Willoughby carrying the garbage out one evening to the smokeless burner behind the house. Singular, yes; Betsy Gifford, who spotted this phenomenon, pronounced herself as stunned as if she had discovered him dancing around a Maypole without benefit of clothes.

Because Jason Willoughby was simply not a man who carried out garbage—or washed the car or trundled heavy bags of groceries or lifted a finger in the small vegetable garden; not when he had a devoted wife to do all these things for him. To call him selfish and demanding was like describing a hurricane as breezy.

Even the other husbands of Earlsgate Crescent, who might have been expected to salute him, however furtively, were disapproving. Great selfishness had to be offset by vast charm if it were to be tolerated at all, but Jason Willoughby—a handsome thirty-five with an expensive-looking droop to his eyelids—always managed to convey the impression, on social occasions with his neighbors, that he was honoring an impulsive and ill-conceived promise.

On the other hand everybody liked Margaret Willoughby—except Charles Hunt, who loved her. He had managed to keep this fact a secret by not avoiding her and by taking out the girls foisted on him by well-meaning matrons. The girls were frequently attractive, but none of them had Margaret's beautiful nearsighted gray-blue eyes with the frankly thirty-two-year-old lines at the corners, or her fierce and misplaced dedication. The girls were deft and sure-handed; you would never catch them adorned with Band-Aids or other running repairs. Why he should have found accident-prone Margaret so lovable Charles could not have explained, but he found her just that.

It came down to a very basic equation: Margaret loved Jason, Charles loved Margaret, Jason loved Jason—and here, all of a sudden, was Jason performing menial tasks.

Why?

There was a good deal of speculation in the Crescent, especially on the Saturday when Jason was seen washing the car. Betsy Gifford said, "Maybe Margaret's been left a lot of money. *That* would make his heart beat faster"; and Dr. J. Hughes Foster, who was an obstetrician and tended to think in only one direction, said, "Obvious. She's pregnant."

But these two theories were swiftly disposed of. Margaret's parents were dead and she was an only child; there was no one to leave her money. Betsy Gifford, who was expecting a baby in November, made circuitous approaches and learned that Margaret was not pregnant. "Maybe," said a starry-eyed new resident admitted to these councils, "Mr. Willoughby just did some, you know, soul-searching, and decided to turn over a new leaf."

"Jason Willoughby in search of his soul," said Charles's landlady trenchantly, "is on a fool's errand."

In early July attention turned elsewhere: the Van Burens' son, who had been an Eagle Scout, came shambling home from his first year of college and a round of visits to relatives in the Southwest with hair like long black Brillo, jeans with spectacular rents, a disconcerting habit of rocking his shoulders and snapping his fingers as he talked, and a female companion with owlish glasses and large bare feet.

Charles had a moment of entertainment when he thought the girl would look well loaded with panniers, then went back to a notion that filled him with terror. Margaret *seemed* well, tanned if a little thinner from her gardening efforts, but suppose—

No, Jason Willoughby wasn't a monster. If Margaret had been to a doctor and received some terrible prognosis, even Jason would have changed his habits. Oh, God, thought Charles, watching Jason tie up tomato plants with the clumsy motions of someone new to it, that must be it.

He lay in wait, because this was an area in which he wanted his reassurances first-hand. His apartment was three houses away from the Willoughbys', and, as a writer, he had the advantage of being constantly in residence. He was there on an afternoon heavy with thunder when Margaret drove by. At first she appeared to have a passenger beside her; memory translated that into a great heap of clothes from the cleaner's.

Charles shot out of his apartment, sauntered the rest of the way, and was at the car in time to say casually, as Margaret ducked inside, "Can I give you a hand with that?"

"Oh, hello, Charles, would you?" Her dark hair was shiny even in this subdued and threatening light, the whites of her eyes snowy in the grateful glance she gave him. Charles wondered absurdly what she would do if he asked her to stick out her tongue. Her right wrist was bandaged, as was so often the case, and as though she felt his clinical attention she said, "The handle of the iron came loose when I wasn't expecting it. I burned a gigantic hole in one of Jason's best shirts."

Well, of course. Jason Willoughby would not descend to no-iron shirts like other men. Come to that, most if not all the clothes inside the slippery transparent bags were masculine—was he planning on a trip? A long one?

Charles was still turning that over in his mind when Margaret used her key and said, "Thanks very much— just dump everything on the couch and I'll put them away later," and consulted the clock. "Jason ought to be home any minute. You'll have a drink, I hope."

Charles said he would; he was determined to quell his own fears if possible. All the subtle approaches he had planned fled out of his head at the sight of Margaret tranquilly getting out an ice tray and three glasses as if—forget the third glass—as if it were natural and right for them to be alone at this relaxed end-of-the-day moment. Relaxed? He was so tense with the effort of not getting up to be beside her in that small space, to put his hand over hers as she lifted down bottles, that blank seconds went by until Margaret said, like throwing a lifeline, "How's your sister?"

Barbara had come to visit him in the spring, and she and Margaret had liked each other at once. "Fine. Trouble is," said Charles, regaining a measure of cunning, "she's just had her annual checkup and now she's after me to have one, although I've told her I'm sound in wind and limb."

"Well, you know," said Margaret, pouring Scotch, "it isn't a bad idea. I know it's a horrible nuisance and they certainly don't do it for nothing, but Jason shipped me off for mine a month ago and it's sort of reassuring to know everything's in order and working."

Charles could almost have closed his eyes with relief, but was glad he didn't. At the sound of a slammed car door in the driveway Margaret said, "Here's Jason," and something extraordinary happened to her face; it became electrical and—driven? As though every tiny muscle responded to a summons, so that her cheekbones became higher, her eyes wider, her skin more taut. It might have been pleasure and expectation; to Charles, who had never seen her awaiting her husband before, it looked unavoidable, like the answer to a challenge.

Jason, his seersucker jacket hooked over his shoulder until Margaret sprang to put it on a hanger, greeted Charles with the cordiality he might have extended to an insurance salesman at the end of a long hot harassed day. He shot a penetrating look at the glistening burden on the couch, picked it up, and walked through an inner door with it, then came back to say handsomely to Charles, "Finish your drink," as though that might be Charles's last chance at a cocktail for the foreseeable future.

Charles didn't finish it. Mission accomplished, he said to himself as he walked home. There was nothing wrong with Margaret's health and she had had her checkup at her husband's urging. All as it should be, so why did he feel that there was something—gathering in that house?

Instinctively, almost superstitiously, he glanced at the sky, and a trickle of frozen silver flashed through the plummy clouds overhead and was followed almost at once by more thunder and the first missile-like drops of rain. He actually stopped in his tracks and half turned before he convinced himself that he was a nervous fool, that nothing had just exploded in that calm and pretty room.

On Saturday Jason did the grocery shopping.

It was doubtful if he had bought so much as a quart of milk since his marriage, and Charles watched him in amazement from the partial shelter of a magazine rack. Jason proceeded along the shelves like a man in a minefield, wheeling his basket in a fashion at once demeaned and haughty, picking up cans and examining the labels as though they were written in a foreign language. The meat department seemed to hold special bafflements, and after toying indecisively

with a number of packages he leaned across the
counter and apparently sought advice from a butcher.

It never entered Charles's head to walk boldly out
of concealment and accost Jason. He wished briefly
for the presence of, say, Sue Cassidy, the latest of
the girls introduced to him by Betsy Gifford. Sue
was very serious-minded—whenever Charles looked
deep into her melting brown eyes he seemed to see
tiny brisk messages there, like "Have you voted?"—
but she didn't *look* serious-minded and she could have
wheedled some explanation from Jason.

Jason had become tired of wheeling his basket
around. He abandoned it impassably in the middle
of the aisle and departed in a direction which would
take him to relishes and salad dressings. Charles left
the magazine rack at such speed that he stepped cruelly on the sandaled foot of a woman in curlers, apologized perfunctorily to a face dumb with anguish, and
made a rapid inventory of Jason's basket, a thing he
considered offensive when people did it to him. Paper
plates, a package of ground round, hamburger rolls,
mustard, pickles—all suggestive of a picnic.

But Jason's Sundays were devoted exclusively to
golf.

Charles escaped down an aisle strangely labeled *Coffee, Tea and Insecticides,* and at the checkout counter
bought a pair of sunglasses that closely resembled
Margaret Willoughby's. Ten minutes later he was
holding them out to her on the shadowed front lawn,
saying, "I saw these on the sidewalk when I was driving by. They're yours, aren't they?"

"No," said Margaret at once. "Mine are prescription, but thanks very much anyway. I'm as blind as a bat beyond ten feet."

"I owe you a drink," said Charles, watching her face carefully. "Maybe you and Jason could come over at noon or so tomorrow?"

"We can't, thanks, Charles, we're going to the beach." Her eyes were so brilliant they looked almost dazed—was that the heat, or surprise because for once her husband was going to devote a portion of the weekend to her? "It's supposed to be hot again tomorrow, and high tide's at around two. We're going to cook out on the rocks."

"Maybe next week then," said Charles, and went home with his false sunglasses.

"Howie Van Buren and that girl have run off to California," reported his landlady when he delivered the pound of butter she had commissioned him to buy.

"She's got good feet for grape trampling," said Charles absently. "I saw Jason Willoughby at the store, by the way."

"Did you now," said Mrs. Spain deeply. "Well, I think I've figured that out. You know how he's never home on weekends? Suppose he's not golfing but off with a lady friend, and Margaret found out about it and threatened to leave him? He's a man who likes his comfort, God knows, and he'd never find another woman to fetch and carry for him the way she does. All these errands are instead of candy and flowers. If you ask me, Howie Van Buren is on marijuana or something worse. His poor mother said she saw him talking to a cat for five minutes."

"The time to really worry is when she hears the cat talking back," said Charles.

Ironically, he felt almost lighthearted at Mrs. Spain's explanation of Jason Willoughby's odd behavior. A man of such ego would feel threatened indeed by the possible loss of such a tireless, dedicated wife and might well hope to woo her back by taking on alien labors like gardening, car washing, and shopping.

And here Charles had been thinking—he could spell it out to himself now—that there had been something infinitely chilling in the air, something that endangered Margaret's very life.

Sunday was hot again, as predicted. Charles found himself telephoning Sue Cassidy and suggesting the beach, because somehow two people in such a scene were more invisible than a lone man, and felt absolved of any guilt whatever when Sue, ravishing in a strawberry-strewn terry robe which suggested no bathing suit at all underneath, insisted on first dropping off political flyers to volunteers at three supermarkets. "Boyd is going to be a *marvelous* man for District Three," she confided, and Charles said, "Good. Great," with the heartiness of the nonlistener.

Because during the night, he had looked at the other side of the coin. *If* Jason Willoughby had an extramarital interest and Margaret had found him out, she would reject divorce with the flatness of a mother rejecting an institution for a retarded child. What she felt for him might not be love, by now, but the deep and damaging habit of a phonograph needle caught in a groove with no one to lift it out. In any case she would wait out an affair, stoically—but what if Jason didn't want her to wait?

Margaret was accident-prone, as everybody knew. People would be shocked but not incredulous if she dived too deep or missed her footing on one of the massive rocks that made an arm curving into the Sound and hit her head fatally.

But then why everything that had gone before?

Charles had almost caught it at some pre-dawn hour, when he had wakened damp and shaken at an unthinkable pattern very clear to see if you looked at it from the right perspective. Not money, not material gain . . . A cigarette had only served to drive it further away, and by morning he had nothing to go on but the conviction that he must be here on the beach, because he was certain Jason had completed his preliminaries.

Was Margaret aware? Was she walking half-willingly toward her doom?

"Why are we at this end of the beach?" asked Sue crossly, stepping over the shell of a horseshoe crab in Charles's determined wake. "We don't have to cook, I've brought sandwiches."

With fires discouraged on the beach itself, the rocks were for the most part the refuge of families preoccupied with their lunch and their young. A good deal of lotion applying went on, and slapping of small hands away from marshmallows before the ritual toasting, and settling of quarrels among children cranky with the heat, and admonitions to the older ones to look after the younger ones when they ventured down onto the little arc of beach below the rocks. This was where the adult eyes would be drawn, to cries of "Watch me! Watch me!" followed by handstands in the shallow water.

Charles thought about all this as he pretended not to hear Sue. He stared out along the arm of rocks, seeing a lone and unattended fire there, seized by fear that gave him an actual pain in his chest. (Margaret, to Jason: "Charles asked us for a drink but I told him we were going to take our lunch to the beach." Jason, carelessly, as the morning deepened: "Why don't we go right now?")

Sue and her flyers . . . and then, just as Charles was finding it difficult to breathe, Margaret's white-capped head in the water almost at the point of the rocks. Inexplicably, unless he had been there in the sun dazzle all the time, a strange swimmer appeared, farther out, a dark-goggled, beige-capped man who had no business being so far from shore; his stroke was weak and wide.

Nothing like Jason's powerful crawl.

The beige-capped man had evidently realized his predicament, and so had Margaret; when the dark-goggled head disappeared briefly she reversed direction and struck out after him, her arms cutting strongly through the silvered glisten of the water.

The glisten . . .

"I'm as blind as a bat beyond ten feet . . ."

Sue must have said something plaintive about a hardboiled egg, but Charles only translated and discarded it after he had surfaced from a shallow running dive. Although he tried to close his mind to everything but getting the maximum effort from heart and lungs, arms and legs, the thought slipped through that a man who had been planning for weeks to kill his wife might have come to believe that his victim would avoid him in the water.

And there were fatalities every summer, when panicky swimmers dragged their would-be rescuers down. Discard the cap and goggles, appear to be too late to save his wife, pretend to hunt furiously for the irresponsible stranger who had brought about her death—

Charles rounded the point, lungs protesting, air tasting literally sweet when he gulped it in, and came upon Jason, his hand braced firmly in a crevice of rock, holding Margaret patiently underwater against its slippery side with the full strength of his leg.

In spite of Jason's bent-bow position his attitude looked quite calm, that of a man with nothing to fear from observation by a few seagulls. An oyster boat was a barely discernible outline on the horizon, and the buffeting wind and seethe of surf here had deafened him to any approach.

Charles trod water, filled his lungs again searingly, clipped a forearm against Jason's throat with all the force he could muster, pushed savagely, and dove for Margaret. Hand braced where Jason had braced his, he had to slap her hard between the shoulders before she began to choke out water and gasp.

Jason had surfaced again. "That was close," he said breathlessly. "I—"

Charles was still heaving for air, but he managed

to say, "If you come near her again I'll kill you."

He didn't watch Jason swim away—with what tale? Charles found a rock outcropping to hang onto and moved Margaret's hand to the crevice where his had been, because neither of them could attempt the return to shore just yet. And Margaret said presently, "He's been so—these last weeks—I think he's mad."

Mad? Charles chose to conserve his breath. Later Margaret would put together for herself the appalling pattern that almost revealed itself to him during the night; but now wasn't the right time.

It was the sheen of the water, reminding him sharply of the glistening cleaner's bags on the couch in the Willoughby house, that had shot it sharply into focus minutes ago. Jason's entire wardrobe, cleaned. His sudden familiarization with domestic chores. He couldn't marry again immediately without arousing talk and suspicion; there would have to be a respectable interlude.

Jason Willoughby, embracing his own comfort as another man might embrace religion, had been practicing to be a widower.

Tiger by the Tail

CONJURING. Always before, in Hugh Trainor's mind, the term had been surrounded vaguely by witch doctors, drums, evil-faced little dolls. After that July, it brought up a sun-stilled country morning at a hospital.

The ivy-grown white building looked more like a home than a hospital—so he and Julia had said when they drove by it two days before on their way to the shore cottage they had rented for two weeks, leaving their house and three small children in the care of a housekeeper.

"Let's have a swim as soon as we get there, before this weather can change its mind," Julia had said as they neared the cottage.

But they didn't, quite. Towel over his shoulder, Trainor paused on the tiny porch to light a cigarette while Julia ran impatiently ahead. She had no time for the conspicuous sign at the top of the steps leading down to the beach: CAUTION. SLIPPERY STEPS. PLEASE USE HANDRAIL.

Trainor heard her sharp gasp, and then a single violent echo of weight on wood. When he got there she lay queerly twisted in the sand, stunned with pain and shock, face stark against the yellow of her rubber cap. Julia had broken her back, or, according to the doctor at the hospital two hours later, that was what it amounted to.

When Trainor went in to see her, his heart gave an appalled bang at the sharp vixen face that turned on the pillow, eyes flaming at him like a caged eagle's, until he realized that there hadn't been a private room vacant and Julia's bed was on the other side of the drawn pink curtain.

He tiptoed around it, surprising a nurse in the act of leaving. Julia was asleep. She looked broken and punished, the bones of her face thrusting against the skin, as though the unfelt pain was taking its toll in some secret way.

On the other side of the curtain, the vixen's voice said demandingly, "That your wife?"

"Yes."

"Pretty bad shape," the vixen remarked.

Trainor could have struck her, even though his ear recognized the accents of the professional ghoul. She couldn't have been more than 35 or so, but she had false teeth which gave an aggressive clash to every-thing she uttered. And perhaps she wasn't even a ghoul; the sharp face, the flatness of the body under the hospital spread, the cynical eyes could very well be reflections of her own pain.

Trainor said temperately, "Not too bad, according to the doctor," and she summed up all doctors and husbands with a look of pitying scorn. Trainor had left . . .

The doctor had said Julia would be drowsy that night, and she was. The next morning her eyes were clear; she had put on lipstick and, with the nurse's help, tied back her shiny taupe-colored hair with a ribbon.

Trainor could not put a finger on what had shocked him about her appearance, just as he could never have defined what gave her face its peculiar and head-turning charm. Was it the faintly sculptured look about her eyelids, the tiny curl of her mouth corners, the spirit of which she had an almost daunting amount?

Whatever it was, it was missing. She said in a flat voice, "It's not as bad as it looks, really, but there goes your vacation. I could kick myself."

"Think so?" said Trainor, and then, "I haven't found a library yet, but I brought you some magazines."

Julia's finger strayed to the top of the pile and dropped away. She said, "Maybe it's lying in this position but I don't feel particularly like reading. Mrs. Emilio could probably use some of these."

"Mrs. Emilio sure could," said the voice from around the curtain, and Trainor left his chair and took her the magazines. He had a depressed feeling that she would listen to every word they said anyway, and an even more depressed feeling that they wouldn't say anything the whole hospital couldn't hear. Julia was listless as well as remote—a hangover from the drugs? Physical shock, or the subtler shock to her confidence?

She said when he came back, "I hope you didn't give up the cottage."

"Of course I did—it's over an hour's drive from here."

"But you paid the whole two weeks," said Julia,

with her first glimmering of reaction.

"They settled for half, and it doesn't matter anyway. I've taken a room within walking distance of
here."

The normal Julia, fascinated with people and
places, would have asked instantly, "Where? Who
with? What's it like?" But instead she said without
interest, "I suppose it is easier for you, not having
to drive back and forth. But what a way to
spend . . ."

Her voice would have trailed off even if the nurse
had not brought her breakfast just then, Trainor
thought. While Julia fiddled with scrambled eggs,
looked blankly at her toast, and sipped at the coffee
she usually drained with zest, he watched her with
a deepening anxiety. If she would only complain
about the food, or make one of her indescribable faces
in the direction of Mrs. Emilio's bed; if she would
only launch into a spirited attack about being wakened at dawn, as she must have been, to be washed
and thermometered and then left to wait interminably
for breakfast and morning visiting hours . . .

But she did not, and the docility frightened him
almost as much as the injury had.

Beyond the dividing curtain Mrs. Emilio's visitors
had arrived in a babble of greetings, a scraping of
chairs, a final settling of feet. They were a man and
woman, their voices hoarse and vivid, pointing up
Julia's—not boredom, because boredom was a positive
thing—total lack of interest. She didn't give Trainor
the rapt look he expected; instead, her gaze moved
absently away and she asked him for a cigarette.

He said as he lit it, "I called Mrs. Castle in case she tried to get us at the cottage. The kids are fine, and it seems we have a pet toad to look forward to."

Julia smiled flickeringly, and he was encouraged.

"They're currently on the trail of some garbage to put out to catch flies for the toad, but Mrs. Castle said nothing doing."

"Killjoy," said Julia, but the brief spark had gone out.

There couldn't be any damage to her nervous system, or the doctor would have told him. Was it reaction to the terrifying fall, some unfaced fear about getting on her feet again, an instinctive recoil from even mental effort? Or simply a natural depression at having their long-awaited vacation spoiled. If there was only something to distract her mind.

Unbidden, but unerring after eight years of marriage to Julia, Trainor's own mind supplied him with the something.

He said very casually to Julia's window-gazing face and aimlessly plucking forefinger, "I've landed with a queer pair of birds." His conscience smote him, but not very hard. "More than queer, if you ask me."

It was as simple as that. In bird-twittered sunlight, without witch doctors or drums or evil-faced little dolls, the thing was done.

Hearteningly, in the second before he bent to kiss her goodbye Julia's glance was wakened and thoughtful . . .

Trainor went swimming, feeling callous about it, and lunched on steamed clams and cold beer at a small waterside restaurant. Any smallest contrition he felt on behalf of the Kingsleys he put instantly out of his head. They would never know they had been presented to Julia like a tangle of wool to be unraveled. Julia would start to puzzle alertly over the problem, and everybody would benefit.

He telephoned the hospital after lunch and found that Julia would be having x-rays during the afternoon visiting hour, which left the day suddenly open. His small room at the top of the Kingsleys' maple-darkened house held no appeal. In the end he took himself to an air-conditioned horror movie.

The director, he found himself thinking in the popcorn-crunching dark, had none of Julia's subtlety in this direction. The villains here were forthright, and everybody knew at a glance that these waxen, stiffly walking characters were not the best of citizens. Julia's villains, on the contrary, were always sterling members of society.

When he reached the hospital the warm night was black. Julia was better, and his heart lifted at once. The indefinable quality was back, the thing that made people turn to look at her; it was as though she had come out from under an eclipse.

She said, "It's not as bad as they thought, and the doctor thinks I'll be able to go home in a week. I'll have to wear some sort of contraption at first, and we'll have to keep Mrs. Castle on for a while . . . but what about these people you're with? What's their name?"

"Kingsley."

"How did you happen to land there?"

And she was back. She had been gone, but she was back.

Trainor kept his elation to himself. He explained that as there was no hotel most of the houses in the neighborhood of the hospital had a room or rooms to rent; he had been to five, all bespoken by relatives of patients, before a woman told him to try the Kingsleys. "They don't rent as a rule, but they have the room and I'm sure they wouldn't turn you away under the circumstances. I'm Mrs. Stuart—tell Mrs. Kingsley I gave you her name."

Trainor would certainly not have got in without that talisman. The house Mrs. Stuart had indicated was set back from the street, tall and white, its inelegant lines, in a landscape full of graceful houses, partly concealed by maples and pines.

The woman who opened the door at his ring was prepared to be firm; Trainor could see her gathering breath for it. He said at once and disarmingly, "Blame Mrs. Stuart, she sent me here," and after a considering moment the door opened wider.

Mrs. Kingsley was disconcerting in every respect. She was perhaps sixty, short, heavy, and shapeless, but she had an air of hauteur in a faded housedress and slippers. Her face was baggy and wrinkled inside its short, sparse lavender hair, but there again a pair of very pale, shrewd green eyes belied the country-woman appearance. Her voice was the most startling thing of all—alto, almost aggressively educated, and set at the next-to-breaking pitch in which accomplished singers speak a song rather than sing it.

She listened attentively to the tale of Julia's misfortune, although her gaze had long since summed Trainor up and decided. She said when he had finished, "You poor young man. Of course I'll have to ask Mr. Kingsley, so if you'll excuse me for just a minute . . ."

Mrs. Kingsley said a little later as she led the way up the stairs, "You may not like the room at all, Mr. Trainor. It's a converted attic—" they were on a second and shorter flight of stairs now, and she had begun to puff "—and there's no use saying you won't get the heat under the roof, because you will. That's why we don't usually consider it a room to rent, and then too—" she had opened a door now, and preceded Trainor inside with an odd air of challenge "—it was our boy's."

Something about her tone precluded any kind of polite inquiry, and Trainor took refuge in an attentive turning-around inspection of the small steep-ceilinged room. There was only one window, letting in leafy light on a bed and bureau and straight chair. A microscope stood on the bureau top—"I'd rather you didn't touch it—you see it's focused just so," said Mrs. Kingsley firmly—and a camp banner and baseball glove hung limply from one wall.

The sun seethed down from the roof.

"Twenty dollars a week," Mrs. Kingsley said at length, and managed to combine firmness, apology, and scorn for the $20 all in one breath.

"Done," said Trainor. He regretted it faintly even as he produced his wallet. The room was small and hot and hung pervasively with memories; but he was tired and anxious to have a base of operations . . .

Julia listened with wide attentive eyes. These were malefactors after her own heart, quiet people, immensely cunning, who paid their taxes and water bills promptly, and probably belonged to civic organizations. "What does Mr. Kingsley do?"

"He's a retired C.P.A., I gather, gone into real estate. There's a discreet sign on the lawn, behind several pines."

"And what makes you think . . . ?"

"Ah," said Trainor deeply. He had been expecting this, and had thought of a number of dramatic peculiarities with which to endow Kingsley; but he fell back on a suddenly remembered truth. "For one thing, he drove up in the small hours of the morning with his headlights off. He could hardly have been showing houses at about three A.M., and why no headlights?"

"Because he's afraid of his wife," said Julia dampeningly. "He'd been playing poker or having a few drinks with some old cronies, and hoped to sneak in."

"No, because they had a long talk after he came in. They're not under me—there's an empty room there," Trainor's brow wrinkled briefly; "but Mrs. Kingsley has a carrying voice and I'd have heard any kind of argument. She was obviously up and expecting him. Anyway, he went downstairs again afterward. It must have been three-thirty or so."

"And when did he come up?"

"I fell asleep."

"Idiot," said Julia tenderly. "I wouldn't have fallen asleep. I'd have been up there chafing my wrists or slapping my cheeks as the case might be. What about this boy she mentioned? Is he dead, do you suppose?"

Trainor thought back to the challenging, oddly pitched voice and frowned again. "I'd think yes from the way she spoke, but the fact that they keep that room as it is . . ."

"He'd be a good thirty at least by now," said Julia practically, "and hardly interested in the baseball bat or whatever it is, or the microscope. If there were really anything going on, any middle-of-the-night business they couldn't afford to have anyone see, they wouldn't have let you have the room in the first place."

"They'd have had to unless they wanted to call attention to themselves," said Trainor without conscious thought.

"Odd that they put the boy at the top of the house when there's a vacant room on the second floor—or is it? No," said Julia, obviously to herself, "it isn't. Boys like rooms like that . . ."

On the other side of the pink curtain Mrs. Emilio's visitors arrived with cries of greeting and cracklings of wrapping paper. Trainor's horrified ear presented him suddenly with the memory of a complete and attentive silence before that. It was one thing to spin tales for Julia's entertainment; it was another to spread gossip and suspicion about people who lived in the town.

Julia's grimace showed him she had thought of the same thing; hastily, although their voices were now covered, she began to talk about something else. But she was still thinking about the Kingsleys when Trainor left—he knew that bright absorbed look. Had he, he wondered half-amusedly, a tiger by the tail?

Guilt pursued him down the hill and through the warm night to the Kingsley house. A long glistening car was parked in front of it, and the lawn was lavish with light.

Trainor would hardly have known Mrs. Kingsley in smart black and white silk, her wayward lavender hair waved and subdued under a small white hat. He was introduced to a pleasant tanned woman and her genial, gray-haired husband; he half expected an introduction to the tall white-coated military-looking man with them until he realized that it was Kingsley, shorn of his shamble and his gardening clothes. They were going out for an evening of bridge. Mrs. Kingsley left a single lamp burning in the living room and then they were gone, the Kingsleys' car following the other car.

Trainor mounted the stairs to his room and undressed. The Kingsleys certainly had nothing to hide, or they would not have left him, a total stranger, in sole possession of the house. The thought passed seriously through Trainor's mind until he recognized it for one of Julia's and threw it out with irritation.

It came back. He realized that, law-abiding though he was, he had a strong sense of privacy and he would have hesitated to leave a stranger at liberty in his own home.

On the heels of that came the thought that if he *had* something to hide, and wanted to test the stranger, he would do exactly as the Kingsleys had done: drive trustingly away, allow time for temptation to take hold—and then drive quietly back.

Knowing himself to be ridiculous—he would be as bad as Julia soon—Trainor turned off his light. The street was mainly an access to the hospital, and quiet at this hour; the passing cars were infrequent and noticeable. It was perhaps 15 minutes before his suspicions became truth. Then, silent as a cruising shark, the shadow-gray Chrysler, only its parking lights on, returned.

The passenger window rolled down and Mrs. Kingsley's large face emerged, a pale blur tilted up toward the window of Trainor's room. He was instantly back from the sill in a movement which, he realized later, was like the instinctive ducking from a flung stone.

Moments went by before he took a craning step forward. As soundlessly as it had crept up, the Chrysler was slipping away; again and unpleasantly, Trainor was reminded of something searching expertly for prey. He pulled down the shade, turned on the light, and got dressed.

In the morning Mrs. Kingsley had reverted. She was in a shapeless old cotton dress and carpet slippers, her sparse hair disarranged, when Trainor was leaving for the hospital.

"Good morning, Mr. Trainor, and it is a good one, isn't it? Did you sleep well? I hope we didn't disturb you—we had a little trouble with the car and got delayed."

"I didn't hear you at all," lied Trainor, "so your reputation is safe with me."

"It was two ten," said Mrs. Kingsley, looking at him with disconcerting clarity. "I wonder—" She put down the straw basket she carried and lifted from it a bunch of dew-wet, very pale pink roses, "I wonder if you would take these to your wife?"

Julia was abashed too, but said with an innocent air, "Did Mr. Kingsley come back late last night?"

 "Yes. They both did."

"With the headlights off?"

"Yes."

"Hugh, if you're going to tell me that you fell asleep again—"

"I didn't." Trainor glanced with automatic caution under the pink curtain that divided the room. With a warning face at Julia he left out names.

"He went down to the cellar. I could see the light on the grass. She came right upstairs, and he came up about five minutes later."

"The cellar," said Julia, spellbound. Thoughts of an earthen floor, or newly laid concrete, drifted visibly across her face. "You don't suppose . . . ?"

"No," said Trainor hastily. "You don't imagine he'd come home with a different one every night?"

"It might be," said Julia delicately, "in—you know—installments, so to speak."

The gentle sex, thought Trainor, mentally gaping. An arm here, this charming wife of his was thinking, a leg there, perhaps a bit of torso to come. "It's nothing like that—but I did find out something about the boy . . ."

Trainor could not have explained his own mixture of feelings after he had turned on the light and got dressed the night before. Shock was foremost, perhaps because of the stealthy return of the Kingsleys' car, perhaps because they had followed his own thoughts with such uncanny precision.

In the wake of that came the outrage that arises from motives correctly suspected. They thought he would prowl around the house, did they? Furthermore, he hadn't a front-door key—Mrs. Kingsley had explained they were always in and it wouldn't be necessary—which meant that unless he left the house open to the night he was stuck here, without so much as a timetable to read.

Virtuously, Trainor told himself there might be an old magazine tucked away somewhere in the room, and in that case he would not have to go downstairs at all.

There was nothing on the closet shelf. The top bureau drawer held a slingshot and a piece of petrified wood with a fading legend: "Souvenir of Arizona, 1945." In the second drawer—they ought not to have left it here if they didn't want it looked at—was a round leather studbox, torn in places, obviously a discard. Trainor opened it without a qualm and looked at a faded newspaper clipping.

The dateline was New Mexico, and the story was terse. "As an army helicopter hovered above Toros Peak today, hope grew fainter for a 16-year-old boy missing on the mountain since Thursday. Stephen Kingsley, son of Mr. and Mrs. Richard Kingsley, Oak Park Place, had gone on a lone camping trip with supplies for only 48 hours. According to search authorities, heavy rains and sharply falling temperatures have lessened the boy's chances for survival on the desolate peak.

"Police here are currently investigating the anonymous telephone call which informed Kingsley's parents the boy was hurt and the caller would lead them to him after $2,000 in small bills had been left in an agreed rendezvous. Mr. Kingsley told reporters he left the money and waited in vain for the message. Mrs. Harriet Kingsley, 49, collapsed and is under a doctor's care."

Trainor dropped the clipping back into the box with a feeling of finality. Small wonder the Kingsleys were suspicious after the cruel maneuver; small wonder that, all the way across the country, they had hung up the glove and the camp banner. Hope sprang eternal, and barring the recovery of their son's body, they would always leave that particular door open.

He was stretched on his bed in darkness, chastened, when a tiny detail came to nag at him. Once again, he turned on the light and opened the bureau drawers.

The slingshot and piece of petrified wood wore a faint, even coating of dust. The leather studbox was shiningly free of it. So—the conclusion came laboriously because there seemed so little point to it—the leather box with the clipping in it had been put there for Trainor to find . . .

"They want you to know about the boy," said Julia, "but they can't bring themselves to talk about him . . . ? No?"

There were so many arguments against that—chief among them, the fact that people so sensitive on the

subject would never have rented that particular
room—that Trainor only shook his head. The Kingsleys had obviously accepted the fact of their son's
death or they would not have moved nearly 3,000 miles
away from the scene of his disappearance—but then
why, in showing him the room, had Mrs. Kingsley
said, "It was our boy's"? Had she meant a comparable
room in another house, or could grief and the un-
changingly boyish possessions have deluded her into
a belief that Stephen Kingsley had, in fact, once occupied the room?

Julia said recallingly, "Hugh," and he realized with
surprise that he had stepped back a day in time, when
she was so frighteningly withdrawn and the night
outside the hospital had looked, because of a ceiling
of green-gold leaves overhead, more like the jungle
than safe, quiet New England.

Something else had happened in the interim. Mrs.
Emilio had two visitors. Crackling went on, as of paper bags, and presently the pink curtain between the
beds gave an imperative twitch.

"Here," said Mrs. Emilio's voice commandingly,
and as neither woman could move in bed, Trainor
poked his head around the curtain, said, "Thanks very
much" to a man with a dark, disarming monkey-face,
and accepted a small wax-papered square.

Unwrapped, it was a rissole of some sort. They
talked about the children as they ate and it was not
until Trainor stood up to leave that Julia said suddenly, "The thing to do is get into the cellar. If he
goes down there after those trips, that's where it is."

"And I could always say," said Trainor dryly, "that

I was passing the cellar window and thought I'd drop in."

Julia was unruffled. "She's a sociable soul, according to you, and if he even makes a pretense of being in the real estate business, he must be out sometimes. You could say you'd smelled smoke, or oil—"

"Or something fishy." Trainor bent to kiss her, and Julia reminded him in a murmur to give Mrs. Emilio the roses on his way out. She didn't glance at the arched and pearly heads. "All of them," she said.

There was a telephone booth in the downstairs lobby, and Trainor stopped on impulse and called Mrs. Castle. It was a lengthy, cops-and-robberish call, and he ought to have been faintly embarrassed about it but—so well had he done his original work—he was not.

There was some kind of theory that advised the puzzler to strip the puzzle down to the known facts, because whatever conclusion they pointed to, however unlikely, was the true one. Trainor, walking down the hill from the hospital, concerned himself with this.

The central fact was that the Kingsleys wanted him to know not that they had had a son—Mrs. Kingsley had volunteered that before he even took the room— but what had happened to the boy.

Why, when they had never seen Trainor before and, after the space of a few days, would in all probability never see him again?

Try it subjectively instead of objectively. In this light the Kingsleys wanted to be established as the bereaved and cruelly tricked parents of a son. But as before, why? Trainor began to speculate, and forced himself back to known facts.

The Kingsleys did not rent rooms as a rule; the neighbor who had directed him there had been positive about that.

Although they had moved from the southwest to New England, they had hung in one small room—a room he had never been in—their son's boyish trophies. Again Trainor wondered why that did not strike him as pitiful but subtly unpleasant.

Twice to his knowledge their car had returned surreptitiously and late, only its parking lights to guide it. On the second occasion it had circled back to check up on Trainor: there could be no other explanation for that noiseless approach, that thrusting of Mrs. Kingsley's face up at his darkened window.

Those were the facts. Also a fact was that people who took pains to plant an impression usually did so for a very real reason—the reason being that the truth was a total variance with the appearance of truth.

Kidnaping—the suggestion that no parent is ever totally armored against—floated through Trainor's mind and vanished. It wasn't a tribute to the Kingsleys but a conviction that, in this close and gossipy neighborhood, it would be impractical. Some fringe of the notion lingered like a mosquito, however; there were innumerable histories of people warped by grief who made a life work of trying to make society pay for an individual loss.

Or else, thought Trainor, the Kingsleys were merely eccentric and that was the explanation.

The sun shone gently, shadows flowed over mown lawns, the Kingsleys could not possibly have turned into an evil pair simply because he had spun a mystery for Julia. And where had that horrifying notion come from?

Once again, he was obscurely relieved to find visitors at the Kingsleys', this time in a handsome dove-and-deep-gray station wagon. The front seat was occupied; a trim elderly woman dressed for golf was being handed into the back by a genial sports-coated man, leather-elbowed, who might have stepped out of a whiskey ad.

It took Trainor a moment to realize that he had just looked at the third aspect of the Kingsleys. They were not two identities, but six—the slippered housewife and the shambling gardener, the precisely groomed woman and the military man, the casual golfer and the tweedy country squire—and how many more?

Trainor reminded himself over his instant thump of shock that Julia, embroiled with the children, wearing a few badges of strawberry jam or most of the baby's bath water, could somehow disappear for half an hour and reappear looking as though she had never washed a dish or changed a diaper in her life.

But—and the difference was hard to define, even to himself—she had been Julia throughout, her gestures and bearing and whole identity unaltered by what she wore or what she was doing.

Whereas, near as he had been to them, intent though he was, he had not at first recognized either of the Kingsleys.

"I'm a golf widower today," said Kingsley pleasantly as the station wagon drove off. If his own plans had been changed by Trainor's appearance on the scene, there was no sign of it. The long rubbery face that had gazed morosely at the floor when Trainor had first seen it now sprang readily into attitudes of amiability; the tufty gray brows moved up and down as though controlled by invisible strings, imparting a keen and twinkling air to the cold gaze beneath. "How is Mrs. Trainor this morning?"

"Much better, thanks." They were sauntering up the walk now, entering the house. "As a matter of fact, the doctor thinks she'll be able to leave the hospital in about a week. Of course, she'll have to have help with the children just at first."

"Oh, of course. Three young children . . . keep her hopping, I imagine."

Was Kingsley very faintly British today?

"We thought," said Trainor, "that the children might be more easily managed—new interests and so forth—in a cottage or some place here. Would you have any summer rentals we could fit into? There'd be my wife and me and the children and a housekeeper . . ."

He ended up, as planned, in Kingsley's office on the other side of the small front hall. It was as tree-darkened as the living room, with desk and file cabinets suspended in gloom. There was a phone on the desk, and a memo pad and pen were neatly aligned on the blotter; but it was impossible to believe that many real-estate transactions went on here.

The files were genuine enough. With an air of recollection that suggested he hadn't looked at them in some time, Kingsley pursed his lips, meditated, drew out cards. "Most of the summer rentals are gone, you understand, but occasionally there's a cancellation, or a tenant isn't satisfactory . . ."

Trainor found fault, apologetically, with everything listed. The place was too close to the water, too far from the water, there wasn't a porch, a back yard was absolutely essential for the children. The phone he kept staring at was as malevolently silent as though the wires had been cut.

"Well, that's it, I'm afraid," said Kingsley at last. "Unless—wait now, I have a few inactive files, people who had withdrawn their properties from the market . . ."

Where the devil was Mrs. Castle's call? Of course she was busy with the children—or she might have forgotten. She might not even have understood.

". . . and might reconsider," said Kingsley, standing, and the phone rang.

Trainor devoted himself to his cigarette. He didn't need to glance at Kingsley's face to measure the man's sharp interest; the whole room was taut with attention.

"Governor's Lodge Inn at twelve," repeated Kingsley, after an interval of listening. Trainor caught the automatic motion of the lifted wrist watch. "Yes indeed, Mrs. Dunnington. I have two properties in mind, and both have servants' quarters and stables. One has a view of the water that I think you'll—"

Mrs. Castle was playing her part nobly; she cut him off there. Kingsley said eagerly, "Until twelve, then. Thank you, Mrs. Dunnington."

He hung up and wrote busily. Trainor said with an immersed air, "On the whole, I think this three-bedroom place is the—"

"I wonder if you'll excuse me, Mr. Trainor?" Kingsley was already out from behind the desk, plucking cards from a file, pocketing them, adjusting his meticulous tie. "I have a chance to move a really large country estate here and I have—" nobody knew it better than Trainor "—over an hour's drive to make. I'll be free later this afternoon," he was at the door now, "and we can look at whatever properties you'd like to see."

"I could look at this place in the meantime," said Trainor idly. "Drive by it, see if it's what we'd be interested in."

Kingsley's eyes changed—or had a pine bough moved in front of a window, changing the light? "In that case," he said, glancing at his watch again and then very steadily at Trainor, "I'll just give them a ring to let them know you're coming. A little warning, you know."

Within three quarters of an hour Trainor was back. He was careful not to go too rapidly through Mrs. McGovern's bayside cottage, as Kingsley would check up, but he drove like the wind both ways. When he walked back into the house the mantel clock in the living room said 11:40.

He said loudly, "Mrs. Kingsley?" but the noticeable tick of the clock, a spaced drip from one of the kitchen faucets, were answers in themselves.

Trainor progressed to the kitchen, found the door

to the cellar, closed it carefully behind him, and went down the stairs.

Dampness and coolness wrapped around him like a skin, along with the concrete-and-wood-and-oiled-rag fragrance common to cellars. Trainor resisted the temptation to pull an inviting light string and took a comprehensive if shadowy look around.

The cellar was square, except for the corner containing the oil burner, and very tidy. Along the wall to his right was a well-equipped workbench; Kingsley evidently did a lot of his own carpentry and repairs.

Directly ahead, under the small cobwebby window, were some files.

Something creaked, and Trainor froze involuntarily, staring at the ceiling. An old beam? An enterprising mouse? At this point Julia would have squirted a small stream of oil from a can she had foresightedly brought with her, managing to conceal it, or even chew it up and swallow it.

The sound was not repeated. Trainor crossed the concrete floor and pulled out file drawers, A to J, K to O, P to Z. The inactive files Kingsley had mentioned.

But how neat they were, how dustless, for records relegated to the cellar. Trainor took a second and closer look at A to J.

The cards weren't typed, like the listings in the office files, but carefully handwritten. Each card bore a name and an address and a number of symbols, which Trainor stared at blankly. Typical of them was "Bright, Mr. and Mrs. Holton M., Worcester, d 16, 3/22/58, 1500" and "Fox, James K., Springfield, s 24,

7/12/59, 2500." Another card, beginning "Hissop, Mrs. Celeste," was crossed out indecipherably after that.

Trainor stood suddenly and transfixedly still—7/12/59 was only eight days ago.

Above him, on the peculiar knife-edge of sound that divides harshness from musicality, Mrs. Kingsley said, "Is that you, Mr. Trainor?"

What was there about this woman that even the dim shape of her face in darkness, and now the heavy ankles in wrinkled stockings and carpet slippers which were all he could see, sent an immediate and primitive alarm to the senses?

Trainor controlled his impulse to slam the file drawer shut and made himself say in an absent way, "Yes," and pull out another file drawer and bend and sniff. He said alertly over his shoulder, "Smell it?" and walked over to the oil burner.

"Smell what?" Mrs. Kingsley's slippers made soft shuffling noises on the stairs, a lisping sound on the concrete.

"Smoke," said Trainor, sniffing again like a beagle, turning at last to meet the icily pale green eyes. "At least, I could have sworn—"

"I don't smell anything," said Mrs. Kingsley slowly. Her gaze didn't flicker; it seemed to cut a cold straight path through the shadowy light. An elderly woman, heavy, slow-moving, sparse-haired, she was at this moment indescribably menacing. "Do you mean to say you smelled smoke in your room, Mr. Trainor?"

"No. When I came in just now. I'd been to look at a cottage your husband thought might suit us for the rest of the summer, and—" Trainor shrugged apologetically "—having had a fire in my house not so long ago I guess I smell smoke even when there isn't any. I'm sorry, I must have startled you, turning up down here."

"Oh, it was very kind of you," said Mrs. Kingsley. Something about her had relaxed very subtly. "If there had been a spark somewhere, and Mr. Kingsley and I both away—goodness, one doesn't dare think what might have happened."

She was bland again as they emerged from the stairs into the kitchen, and except for his body chemistry Trainor could almost have smiled at the suggestion that, only moments ago, she had constituted danger. "And how is Mrs. Trainor today?" she asked.

"Much better, thanks . . ."

But she wasn't. Trainor arriving at the hospital on the dot of two o'clock found that they had changed Julia's cast and given her something to deaden the resulting pain, so that when he went in Mrs. Emilio held up an arm to warn him off. She conveyed in whispers that Julia was asleep and had better be left that way. Trainor tiptoed obediently around the curtain.

He wished he hadn't. Julia was sleeping, but in a tormented way: he could almost see the seethe of dreams inside her down-turned head. While he watched she flung out a restless hand, grasped at the bedclothes, and drew them close as though something she loved had almost escaped her and been recaptured just in time.

Trainor returned to the Kingsleys'. The Chrysler was back, Kingsley having reached the Governor's

Lodge Inn to find the pre-planned message that Mrs. Dunnington's car had broken down en route and she would have to make it another day.

Trainor did not go in. He got into his car and drove twenty miles to the nearest newspaper office. It was the Baysville *Weekly Courier,* but the masthead announced it served all the shore towns.

Things were dull at the *Courier* when Trainor arrived, and a pretty blonde college girl waved him to a table in the corner of the office and brought him the *Courier* for July 12.

Trainor had expected to have to dig for any connection between James Fox of Springfield and July 12, but there it was on page 2, with a two-column headline over the furry indistinct picture of a young man in a private's uniform. The headline said, "Springfield Attorney Reveals Disappearance, Fears Accident to Son, 24."

S 24. Son, twenty-four? In that case D 16, noted on Kingsley's file card, was a sixteen-year-old daughter.

Trainor skipped rapidly through the newspaper account. James Fox Jr., son of—etc., etc., had borrowed the family car to take his girl to a movie. Engine trouble having developed on the way, he had left the girl in the car and started walking back to a garage he remembered passing about a mile behind. He had never reached the garage; somewhere along that stretch of heavily traveled highway he had dropped completely out of sight.

But not out of mind—not out of Kingsley's mind. Kingsley had neatly filed his name and address and date of disappearance, and followed that with figure, 2500.

$2,500?

The newspaper he was staring at dimmed suddenly for Trainor and became another chronicle of disappearance, this time a yellowed clipping. There was a figure here, too: on the instructions of an anonymous telephone caller, the Kingsleys had paid $2,000 for information that would lead them to their vanished son.

But that had been fourteen years ago and nearly 3,000 miles away. And in any case—

The society editor blinked through her glasses and the pretty blonde came hurrying across the room when the man who had asked so quietly for a back issue pushed his chair back with jarring violence and walked out without a word.

It was close to 6:00 when Trainor parked in the Kingsleys' driveway, got out of the car, and walked scrutinizingly around it, kicking at a rear tire, bending to sight along the wheels as though he were worried about the alignment.

And there, at the back of the Kingsley garage that this view afforded him, were the newspapers he had thought he remembered from a chance glimpse on the day of his arrival. Stacks of them, neatly baled, secured not with twine but, from a random striking of light from a side window, wire.

He could hear the Kingsleys talking in the kitchen when he entered the house. ". . . dwarf dahlias," Mrs. Kingsley was saying, "for that bed under your office window." Kingsley only grunted. Mrs. Kingsley said pursuingly, "Sophia has a whole border of them, and she says . . ." and Trainor went on up to his room, shaken.

He wasn't shaken long. The subtle crawl of his skin drove him to the bureau drawers again, and although he had half expected the studbox to be gone, it was still there. So were the mementoes in the drawer above it. Trainor stood there for a long time, staring, thinking, finally knowing . . .

"What?" repeated Julia at shortly after 8:00 that evening. "Hugh dear, one of us has been drinking, or—say it again."

Trainor repeated his question. "What did your brothers keep in their rooms at sixteen?"

Julia started to say something, glanced cautiously at his face, and stopped in thought. "You mean aside from laundry and unmade beds? Well, let's see, it's hard to . . . Oh, stolen signs, you know the kind. Cut-out girls they pretended to think were hilarious. Nick had a crush on a girl who had a crush on a football player, and he borrowed a set of barbells from somewhere and hid them under his bed for months. Bill—"

"No slingshots?" interrupted Trainor. "No baseball gloves or camp banners?"

Julia gazed at him in perplexity. "Hugh, you know yourself most boys that age would sooner be caught dead . . . oh." She had remembered his room at the Kingsleys', hung with boyish trophies—but they weren't the trophies of a boy of 16. She said with scrupulous fairness, "If it had been a girl they might easily have kept a doll. That doesn't necessarily—"

"A doll, yes. But also her first dance program, or—" Because his own daughter was only nine months old, Trainor foundered there. The Hissop entry in Kingsley's cellar files slid darkly into his mind. *Finished*, said the black cancelling line run through the rest of the information. Dead, gone.

He said to Julia, "What I mean is that parents keeping up a sort of memorial wouldn't . . . freeze a child at well below the age he disappeared at, would they?"

The perturbation of her drug-bound dreams earlier that day touched Julia's face, dimming the bloom and the confidence. She said with a shudder, "I don't know. I wouldn't think so, but I'm nothing to go by as I don't think I could do it at all."

The wet rustle of rain intruded briefly.

"I don't think the Kingsleys did it either," said Trainor.

The telephone summons he had heard from his room had obviously been for Kingsley, because a few minutes later Trainor watched him pause by the Chrysler, shuffle through cards he drew from his inside pocket, and drive away. He was clearly on his way to show a house or houses.

Mrs. Kingsley remained, and after that interlude in the cellar Trainor was sure she would not leave the house while he was in it. He showered and dressed, listening to the first heavy plopping of raindrops on the maple leaves, and presently the sound of a horn in the street below.

A light blue Cadillac stood there. While Trainor watched, the passenger window rolled down and a woman's voice called, "Hi. I wasn't sure you were home. Anything I can do for you downtown?"

Mrs. Kingsley came into view, sheltering her head with a newspaper. Her voice floated eerily from under it. "No, thanks, Alice, but come in, won't you?"

She reached the car and stood leaning in; it was evidently one of those can't-stay, won't-go situations. The raindrops thickened and quickened, and after a moment the ignition was switched off, the door opened invitingly, and Mrs. Kingsley got in and closed the door lightly behind her.

After one all-important pause, Trainor was out of his room and running down the stairs. Mrs. Kingsley would have heard the rush of his shower in the pipes; she couldn't know how rapidly he had dressed. If only she hadn't left something on the stove—

She hadn't. Trainor took the cellar stairs at a reckless pace, counting on the fact that most women lost track of the minutes in conversation. He needed not much more than a minute now that he knew what to look for. Bright, Fox, Hissop—he simply hadn't gone far enough into the files before.

And here it was, expected but inexpressibly shocking in black and white.

"Kingsley, Mr. and Mrs. R., Oak Park, N.M., s 16. 9/4/45, 2000."

Julia said in a whisper, "He wasn't their son?"

"I would bet," said Trainor grimly, "they aren't the Kingsleys. I would bet they're a pair of extortionists living on other people's grief. They don't even have to lift a finger—just read the papers and pounce."

Unconsciously, Julia grasped at something, anything, to resist the truth. "Then what were all these mysterious night trips?"

Trainor shrugged. "Telephone calls to victims, I imagine, from points a safe number of miles from here. All-night diners or gasoline stations . . . even if the call were traced it could never come back to the Kingsleys. And of course they had to keep picking up the money somewhere."

"But—" Julia was still stunned "—people would call the police right away, wouldn't they?"

"Not while there was a chance the tip was genuine. These weren't kidnapings, remember. How could a family be sure they wouldn't land a son or daughter in even deeper trouble by calling in the police? Besides, our friends were very careful. Nobody seems to have been tapped more than once."

"Still—" began Julia, and stopped. Trainor could tell from her pallor that she was realizing how she herself would react if one of the children was missing and she were given a chance to buy information that would find him. She said after a moment, "Why all that business about decorating a boy's room? Why bring up disappearances at all by leaving that clipping in your room? It seems the very last thing they'd do, unless they're completely mad."

"I know," said Trainor slowly. "That's the thing I can't figure out. Except . . . the last man they fleeced was a lawyer. He might have kept his head more than the others; he might have told them that if he were

tricked he had ways of tracking them down. And then
I turned up out of the blue. What better argument,
in case I or anyone else was suspicious, than that
they'd lost a boy and been fleeced themselves? What
looks more pathetic than an elderly couple furnishing
a room for a boy who's obviously been dead for
years?"

"Oh, God," said Julia softly, and Trainor knew
from her evasive glance that she had begun to blaze
with apprehension, that her attention had shot miles
through the rainy night to her own sleeping children.
"Hugh, what are you going to do?"

"I don't know," said Trainor. He suddenly felt
tired. He shook off the lassitude with an effort, along
with a feeling that the Kingsleys would defeat him
in the end and go right on gardening and playing
bridge and preying on the victims of disaster.

He said, "They're hard to get at. They've en-
trenched themselves here, and without actual proof
we're just summer people making a nuisance as usual.
God knows where the real Kingsleys are—abroad,
I'd say, otherwise these people wouldn't have dared
it. I suppose the thing to do is call Fox, as he's the
latest victim, and hear what he has to say. And then
try and convince the local police that the cellar file
has nothing to do with real estate."

"Suppose they destroy the file, or burn what's in
it and substitute a lot of other cards?"

"I got the camera out of the car," said Trainor,
"and propped up a few of the cards and took flash
shots." He could still remember his own wince at
the two lavender-white bursts of light—visible from

the street, through the little cellar window?—that were all he had dared take time for. "I don't know what I got, but the police can do wonders with—"

He had read about the blood draining from people's hearts, and thought it a figure of speech. It wasn't. A kind of automatic caution reasserted itself too late, and he glanced under the pink curtain that divided Julia from Mrs. Emilio.

A pair of thick wrinkle-stockinged ankles uncrossed themselves and a pair of sedate black oxford ties moved out of sight.

Mrs. Kingsley's ankles, Mrs. Kingsley's shoes.

Mrs. Kingsley had been there all the time.

Julia mustn't know. Trainor stood up in the thunder of his blood, all of it concentrated in his throat. He managed to glance at his watch, to say, "Oh, Lord, I told Mrs. Castle I'd call at 8:00 and it's nearly 8:30. Be right back . . ."

Mrs. Emilio's pain-sharp face turned on the pillow as he passed the foot of her bed. Distractedly, Trainor recalled a low nonstop murmur on the other side of the curtain. The murmur covering his voice from all but the fiercest concentration . . .

Trainor must have run to the other end of the corridor, because he ended up breathing fast at the floor nurse's discreetly lighted desk. He gestured at the phone although she wasn't looking at him. "Is that an outside line?"

The nurse continued writing on a sheaf of papers; she said absently, "You'll find a public phone booth in the lobby, sir," and only glanced up when the phone was raked to the edge of her desk, the receiver snatched up, the dial spun.

"I'm sorry, but you can't use this phone." Apology turned to outrage as Trainor gave the operator his home number, holding the instrument well away from her outstretched arm. "I'm sorry, this phone is for emergencies!"

Trainor didn't answer her. He didn't see her. He saw his house miles away, lamplit in the rain, the children asleep. John and Gregory in the room they shared, Mary in her crib. Mrs. Castle mending something, or looking at television . . .

The line was busy.

The floor nurse had advanced courageously around the desk. Trainor crashed the receiver down and ran for the stairs.

He recalled the night Mrs. Kingsley had drawn him in for a highball, the polite questions about his family. Two boys and a girl, wasn't that lovely?

Trainor had reached the lobby. There was only one telephone booth, and Mrs. Kingsley, sedate in lavender and white chiffon, was now emerging from it.

In the outer lobby she put on her raincoat and plastic hood, and produced a small plaid umbrella.

She was walking. Of course she was walking; the Chrysler was elsewhere.

She waited on the stone steps for Trainor with an air of gravity.

"Really, Mr. Trainor, you shouldn't have done that, you know. Give me the film, please."

"I'll give it to Kingsley or whatever his name is," said Trainor over the pound in his throat.

"You'll give it to me. Mr. Kingsley—" she was severe over the name "—is at your home, helping Mrs. Castle get the children dressed in response to your urgent message that they be brought to see their mother at once. Wait," said Mrs. Kingsley at the harsh movement of Trainor's body. "If I call my husband and tell him that I have the film, he'll let you know at once where to pick up Gregory and John and the other one. If you do any telephoning at all . . . oh, I beg your pardon."

She stepped courteously back, gathering her raincoat skirt close as a man and woman emerged from the lobby, while Trainor stared at her, caught in an unreasoning terror by that careless "the other one."

Through a storm of rage and fear Trainor heard Mrs. Kingsley's voice, repeating something from the edged quality of it. "I'm waiting, Mr. Trainor. I'd advise you to hurry up."

Gone was the bland bearing, the almost musical tone of the odd and penetrating voice. Mrs. Kingsley had curbed herself long enough. She was on the verge of trembling, and she seemed, as she had in the cellar, as dangerous as a bared knife.

Trainor stepped silently into the rain, Mrs. Kingsley beside him. They looked, moving off into the darkness, like any pair of hospital visitors—aunt and nephew perhaps.

Trainor suddenly stopped short. "My wife expects me back."

"You can call the hospital from the house and leave a message," Mrs. Kingsley said in a sharp implacable voice. They had reached a street light, and with a deliberate gesture she lifted her wrist to peer at her watch.

He remembered nothing of that silent walk through the rain; all his consciousness was in the tight-closed circle of Julia and the children.

He was so tight that his body had begun to ache by the time they arrived at the Kingsleys' front door. Inside, making Mrs. Kingsley fumble sharply with her key, the phone was ringing.

The sound—just beginning, or about to end?—had for Trainor the perilous quality of an ambulance siren. Just as his clenched hands were losing control, Mrs. Kingsley had the door open, was past him into the dim living room, had snatched up the receiver.

She was not at all an absurd figure for nightmare in her shapeless raincoat and rain-splattered plastic hood. Although she must have been out of breath she marshalled her usual voice to say after an endless pause, "Oh, I see . . . I'll have him—wait, hold on a minute, I believe he's just coming in."

She turned to face Trainor, the receiver a negligent few inches away from her mouth, so that it carried her voice but could not transmit the pale savage gaze above it. "Oh, Mr. Trainor, the floor nurse at the hospital is on the phone. Your wife seems to be upset about you personally."

The receiver changed hands. Trainor stared blindly at the mantel opposite him and said, knowing in a hopeless way that Mrs. Emilio would hear the message at the same time, that everything was fine. There had been some sort of error on Julia's admission form and that had kept him in the office until visiting hours were over; but he would see her first thing in the morning. If you'd just give her that message, and thank you, nurse.

He hung up and turned toward her. "The Kingsleys are dead, aren't they?"

Mrs. Kingsley looked at her watch again. "Get the film, Mr. Trainor. You're going to have quite a drive as it is to collect your—offspring, and until I telephone my husband you won't have the slightest notion of where to go. I'm afraid we hadn't bargained on the rain, so it's possible they'll be somewhat damp. There's nothing to stop you from hitting an old woman over the head, but . . . think of poor Julia."

With Mrs. Kingsley rustling along behind him, he went obediently through the kitchen door to the back lawn.

There was a row of upturned flowerpots under a bench at the side of the house. Trainor's memory had presented them to him when he stood in his room earlier that evening, breathing hard from his race up the stairs and wondering where to keep the film until morning and the re-opening of the town's only camera shop. Not in his room, obviously, and not on his person, because if these people were what he thought, removal of the film could be too easily arranged.

The drenched grass drank up their footsteps; the bench, half in and half out of the waver of light from the kitchen door, was streaming with rain. Trainor bent and reached under the third flowerpot from the left, and there was the film, dry and safe.

Hand it over, because there was nothing else to do. Learn to live with the memory of this cylinder in his hand whenever he turned a newspaper page on a report of extortion ("Mrs. Harriet Kingsley, 49, collapsed and is under a doctor's care.") and remind himself that his children, and through them his wife, had hung in the balance. But what if . . . *what if*—

His left hand, replacing the flowerpot, brushed against another object. He picked it up without sound and straightened in the rain-blurred dark, film in his right hand, and Mrs. Kingsley's arm came out like a striking snake. "I'll take that."

"Wait a minute. You'll call Kingsley right away?"

"Of course. I told you he's been waiting."

With the film in her hand, her voice had lost its cruel edge; she was conciliatory, almost wheedling. That would fit with the wild notion that had just shot through his head—it would fit exactly.

Back into the light from the kitchen, now, with the order reversed: Mrs. Kingsley walking ahead, leaving a wake of triumph; Trainor following, dry-mouthed.

And if he had been right so far, he must be right all the way.

These people weren't killers, but scavengers; not lions, but jackals.

Mrs. Kingsley preceded him through the kitchen into the living room. She seemed oddly hesitant on her way to the telephone there, and she was unprepared for the swift hard seizing of her wrists, the bending upward and backward, so that the film fell to the floor and rolled.

"Call Kingsley, from this number?" said Trainor softly. "Not very likely, is it? Call Kingsley, traceably, at a kidnap rendezvous? Because it would have to be long-distance, wouldn't it? And then you two want a head start, naturally—"

Trainor used his other hand to lay the receiver on the telephone table, dial operator, pick up the receiver again.

She was peculiarly silent as he gave the number of his house, and in the line-drawling silence against his ear it flashed across Trainor's mind that she had won; that they had been forced into a deviation from their usual pattern and he had, ruinously, banked against it. Then Mrs. Castle's serene voice said, "Hello? Oh, Mr. Trainor. The children asked before they went to bed if you were going to call—"

The darkness on the stairs, the reason for Mrs. Kingsley's silence, solidified in a rush that rocked the receiver out of Trainor's hand and onto the floor. The base tumbled after it, landing with a crash and a sharp ping of alarm. Kingsley, a gray-headed mask of light and shadow, was armed with something that moved too rapidly for identification—a table leg?

The little curve-clawed cultivator he had picked up beside the flowerpots sprang into Trainor's hand— a weapon as primitive as his own transition from terror for his children to rage at this monstrous pair. When it had once bitten into Kingsley's corded hand and remained ready at the diving face, Kingsley drew back, panting.

The doorbell rang into the harsh-breathing silence, and rang again. Trainor, who had kept Mrs. Kingsley warily on the edge of his vision, turned his head and saw her pressed against the wall, hair straggling over her wrinkled face.

He said as the doorbell pealed even more insistently, "Come, you have company," and his voice seemed to ricochet around the dim living room. No one, he realized, had spoken a word since Kingsley had sprung out of hiding on the stairs.

But they had been gathering themselves, assessing the danger, finding it real; behind their rigid attitudes and laboring breath they had been consulting each other.

Kingsley hurled the heavy table leg at Trainor's face and lunged for the dining room in what seemed to be one motion. Trainor, twisting his head instinctively and not quite in time, nearly missed the point of the diversion. He got to the film which still lay on the floor just before Mrs. Kingsley's lightning reach, and perhaps because his head was ringing with pain from the glancing blow, he heard with bewilderment a man's voice, evidently raised at Kingsley: "Just a minute, sir!"

The caller had tired of ringing the doorbell, and forced his way in. Mrs. Kingsley's face was a bad color. Trainor turned his head with some difficulty (what in hell was that stick made of?) and looked at a policeman, who was now saying with caution, "There seems to be some trouble here?"

Mrs. Kingsley said with instant indignation, "Officer, this man . . ." and Trainor stopped listening and sat gravely down on a chair, struggling with a wild amusement.

Julia and her midnight hot pastrami, smuggled in
by Mrs. Emilio's myriad relatives and friends, and
the nurse they had suborned among them. What it
came down to was smuggled-in food, smuggled-out
message—to this uniformed policeman whom Trainor
had last met in a dapper blue suit, bowing around
Mrs. Emilio's bedcurtain, at her behest, to convey a
rissole to Julia.

Fox, the Springfield attorney who had been the
Kingsleys' most recent victim, had a wide political
acquaintance. When he had identified Kingsley as the
telephone caller who had promised information about
his missing son in return for a sum of money, phones
were lifted, teletypes busied, newspaper and police
files dug into. Fourteen years and 2,500 miles were
peeled patiently back—to the death by exposure of
a boy on a mountain peak.

There were details which would remain obscure
forever unless the elderly couple now held for extortion chose to explain them, and they showed no sign
of doing so. The inquiry was further complicated by
the fact that the real Kingsleys had lived very much
to themselves even before the death of their son drove
them into deeper retreat. It was known that Mrs.
Kingsley had distant relatives in England and there-
fore assumed, when the house was suddenly closed,
that they had gone abroad.

Certainly no one asked questions; all the questions
had been asked weeks earlier in the search for the
telephone caller who had precipitated Mrs. Kingsley's
collapse. Kingsley had no enemies, and as the boy's

disappearance had been widely publicized throughout
the state, the inquiry hadn't much hope of success.

Now, fourteen years later, the housekeeper who
had known the Kingsleys better than anyone else con-
firmed the fact that they had no enemies; she added,
not surprisingly, that they had had no real friends
either. There had been a childhood friend of Mrs.
Kingsley's (duly checked out and found to be living
blamelessly in Bryn Mawr) and a classmate of Mr.
Kingsley's at college. Down on his luck, so that Kingsley helped him and his wife financially from time
to time.

The housekeeper had been struck by the husband's
resemblance to Kingsley: tall, a little stooped when
he forgot to straighten his shoulders, beginning to
go gray . . . ? Dowd, that was it, Francis Dowd, and
his wife's name was Laura . . .

It was three weeks before Trainor stopped feeling
like a sorcerer's apprentice, and Julia, so she said,
like a West Point cadet in her various straps and har-
nesses. By that time two skeletons had been dug up
from beneath the floor of a fishing cabin in the moun-
tains above Santa Fe, and the man and woman whom
Trainor had known as the Kingsleys had been definitely established as Francis and Laura Dowd. It
seemed unlikely, in view of the mounting file on the
Dowds, that they would ever be free to pursue any
further career.

The summer deepened. The children's toad suc-
cumbed to an overdose of peanut butter, and the house
next door was bought by people named Hathaway.

The Dowds disappeared first from the newspaper, then from daily conversation, and finally from Trainor's consciousness.

Until a night in late August.

The darkness sang with locusts, but there was something else—a muffled and rhythmic sound to which Julia, head turned toward the open living-room window, listened alertly.

"Hathaway," she said after a brooding moment, "banging away on that boat of his—or at least he says it's a boat. It sounds more like an armada."

An expression Trainor was familiar with crossed her reflectively tilted face. She said slowly, "Come to think of it, I met him in the lane the other night, just as it was getting dark, and I happened to think—"

No, thought Trainor; not just yet. It was the sheerest nonsense to imagine even for an instant that conjecture could turn into fact by some black and secret process, and what he felt on the back of his neck was undoubtedly a draft. Still . . . not just yet.

"—what a very open clean-cut upstanding fellow Hathaway really is," said Julia rapidly, meeting his eye. "In fact, let's have a drink on it, shall we, Hugh?"

Something Green
and Growing

ALTHOUGH MONTHS would pass before she surprised its horrifying secret, Mrs. Lear did not care for the plant from the moment she laid eyes on it. And as a Mother's Day gift, of all things.

It was true that, random suggestions as to the altering of any status quo being a way of life with her, she had once remarked that it would be nice to have something green and growing around the house. Pinned down, she would have said something about a pretty hanging basket, but nobody pinned her down. As a result, it was like having made nostalgic reference to a baby and being presented with a truculent teenager.

The plant was very large and flourishing, firmly rooted in a black-vinyl container of suggestive size. Mrs. Lear had seen its ilk in banks and libraries and medical waiting rooms, which guaranteed it as unkillable. Its stem was formidable, its leathery oval leaves a deep green with lighter veining.

"There's a spray you can apply to make the leaves glossy," said Mrs. Lear's son-in-law Leslie, tenderer of this offering.

"But they're so pretty just as they are," observed Mrs. Lear narrowly.

Isabel cast a glance at her mother. "*I* think it's lovely. I don't know whether they like too much sun, so your west window ought to give it the right amount of filtering."

They all gazed at the plant, which now had the grimly determined air of a visitor with time to kill. Coupled with Isabel's earlier present of an ornamental birdbath, and even without the fast flicker of her violet eyes, the message was unmistakable: anyone with these delights to contemplate would happily spend more time in her own quarters.

The quarters were in fact generous: the master bedroom, turned over as a fait accompli by the Gillises in February, with its spacious bath and glass doors opening onto a patio that overlooked a swath of lawn. There were bookcases, and a small desk.

But there was now a hint of captivity, no matter how comfortable, and who knew what might follow— and eventually culminate in, "Isabel, you'll have to do something, your mother is wandering around again"?

In Mrs. Lear, as in most creatures, fear bred anger. "You did say it would grow quite tall, didn't you, Leslie?" she inquired, eyeing the fleshy presence in the pot. "Just over there, I think, beside the piano. That way, we can all enjoy it."

When her daughter had married three years earlier at the unexpected age of thirty-six, Mrs. Lear had gone through all the motions prescribed for widows with only children.

No, she wouldn't live with them, for all their urgings of ample space, and neither would she move to

New Mexico. Both decisions, she assured them, were purely selfish—she was too old to give up her friends, particularly her golfing companions. As to the thousands of miles separating Connecticut from New Mexico, the mail and the telephone existed, and so did the airlines.

Upon which, so scalded by double rejection that for weeks strangers fidgeted uneasily when they became unseen targets of her fixed lavender-ice stare, Mrs. Lear returned alone to her uninteresting house outside Hartford. Leslie Gillis, at forty-nine, was roughly equidistant in age from her and her daughter, and for the first twenty-four hours of the mutual acquaintance formed in Puerto Vallarta, the Lears' annual vacation choice that year, an onlooker might easily have assumed that it was to the elder rather than the younger woman that Leslie was paying his handsome attentions.

It wasn't an outlandish notion. Mrs. Lear was a tallish, tailored woman with pretty eyes, short soft hair whose fawn and grey were sun-blended, features that had been angular in youth but were now aristocratic. By evening they were "Juliet" and "Leslie," while Isabel sat quietly by in the warm, half gilded dark near the swimming pool, the faintly scented air stirring her shoulder-length chestnut hair.

Was it the very tranquility which had drawn such a successful and elusive man—the suggestion that both women were sufficient unto themselves?

Mrs. Lear, who had been left with enough money to live reasonably well with a little management, certainly felt no physical attraction. Isabel, never beset by suitors, had a good many friends among both sexes and a highly paid personal-relations job, involving occasional travel, with a utility company. Neither of them fell upon Leslie Gillis as if he were the only drink of water in miles of desert.

And then suddenly they were together, and Mrs. Lear was alone. We shall see, she said to herself in the very small world which had been emptied of its only real interest. We shall see.

She did not telephone, for all her implied promises, although she talked cheerfully when Isabel did and always exchanged a few amiable words with Leslie as well. Her infrequent letters made reference to ficti- tious people and social involvements, and unfailingly mentioned something which engaged the future.

On the second Thanksgiving of their marriage, the Gillises flew east, providing Isabel with a thorough immersion in nostalgia.

"I had thought of asking a few people in," said Mrs. Lear, nodding at a ranked assortment of un- opened bottles as if her manner had not long since driven away a never-large circle of possible guests, "but then I decided it would be so much nicer to have just us."

In January, having established herself as hale, inde- pendent, and thoroughly unpossessive, she judged the time to be ripe. Borrowing from a narrative overheard in a dress shop, she wrote her daughter that now that it was safely in the past she could describe "My Three Weeks on Crutches," and went on to detail her freakish accident on the stairs, the broken ankle and severely traumatized hip, the doctor's opinion that she had been lucky to get off so lightly.

There were no stairs in the Santa Fe house.

She tracked the letter in its flight, and on the earliest possible evening Isabel telephoned. She said, "Mother. Just listen uninterruptingly for a minute or two, will you? Leslie and I have been talking ever since your letter came this afternoon . . ."

It was as simple as a diagram of the foxtrot. Mrs. Lear gave in gracefully and by February was a permanent member of the Gillis menage in Santa Fe.

The adobe house was on two pinon-clad acres in the hills north of the city, so swept with billows of wind-blown light that for the first week or two dark glasses were a near-necessity. There were huge windows, three patios, a swimming pool. The rugs on the shining deep-red Spanish tile floors were what Isabel described incomprehensibly as Chimayo, mainly grey or mustard-yellow in background, but the big corner bedroom turned over to Mrs. Lear had been newly carpeted in pale-rose broadloom— "just in case," with a smile to take any worry out of it.

Fifty feet behind the house, standing by itself, was the one-room workshop where Leslie, now semi-retired from his investment counseling firm, busied himself with what he called his gadgets. It wasn't entirely a hobby—he had patented and sold a few, chiefly as modifications to small machinery. He had declined to show the workshop to Mrs. Lear on the general tour the day after her arrival: he kept it in a state of uproar and except to another compulsive tinkerer there was really nothing to see. "Besides which," said Isabel with feeling, "the air is full of metal filings or wood dust if Leslie's been near it in twenty-four hours."

Alone with Mrs. Lear, she said, "Don't be shocked, but that place is a godsend. Leslie sometimes spends a whole evening there. I don't know what too much togetherness would do, but I'm much too happy to risk finding out."

It couldn't be denied, even by the most raking scrutiny. Isabel's complexion had always been pale, enhancing the eyes and hair which were her best features, but here in her own house, without travel fatigue, she was positively pearly. Mrs. Lear found all men inscrutable unless they were roaring with laughter or black with rage, but it was clear that Leslie, too, had a single real focus in his life . . .

Mrs. Lear did not at first feel shut out. Although she had no interest in languages not her own and declined Isabel's invitation to attend the small Spanish class that met one afternoon a week, they usually drove somewhere together in the morning. After lunch she took a nap and in the late afternoon joined Isabel in the kitchen to help with vegetable-peeling or sauce-making or whatever else had to be done ahead of time to leave the cocktail hour reasonably intact. It was very companionable—so much so that if Leslie arrived in the doorway it was like the successful approach of a prowler.

When there were people for cocktails, Mrs. Lear stayed, appraising clothes and jewelry and contributing to the edges of the conversation. When it was a matter of dinner to follow, she put forth at the outset the suggestion that she have a tray in her room.

"People would feel that they had to ask me back, and it creates an awkward situation."

Coaxed and wheedled as she had been, and confident that they wouldn't hear of this tiptoeing-relative ploy, she was sharply taken aback at Leslie's light parrying: "But all our friends know you're here, Juliet. We don't want to give the impression that you're chained to your bedstead for the evening."

"I think Mother should do whichever she finds more comfortable when the time comes," said Isabel, almost successful in covering the joking, jarring words. She smiled warmly at them both, as if introducing them to each other. "Heavens, anybody would think we were talking about ground rules for a summit meeting."

By her very defense, the damage was done—under Leslie's always amiable but noticing eye, Mrs. Lear had no option but to hew to her stated intention and exile herself to her room. She did not brood about it; her blood knew very well what might happen if she allowed it to surge free. Instead, she glanced across at the workshop, slantingly visible from her west window, and promised herself, *I will get in there.*

But memory, disciplined, went underground. On an afternoon with the kitchen light on at five o'clock because of a thunderstorm that circled and rumbled, Mrs. Lear was dicing apples for Waldorf salad when Isabel said, with the stiff air of one delivering a message put off as long as possible, "Could you—I know it sounds ridiculous, but could you try not to look startled whenever Leslie makes an appearance? He's quite fond of you, you know, but sometimes you give him the impression that you think he's—creeping up on you."

Mrs. Lear, caught in a pleasant slippage of time in which there were only the two of them, less mother and daughter than friendly peers, thought angrily, Then let him announce himself, and only realized that she had spoken aloud when Isabel, putting washed lettuce in a wire basket, turned her head in astonishment.

She was confused, but only for seconds. "I didn't write you at the time because I didn't want to alarm you," she said, bringing her knife down on an apple core and tossing the tough segments and pits to join the neat little cubes in the bowl, "but a man *did* walk into our house one day when I was still on crutches. He said he'd knocked, although I'm sure he hadn't. He was looking for the Crawfords down the street, but it can be very frightening when you're as good as helpless."

"It would be, of course," said Isabel with patent relief. Take that, Leslie, thought Mrs. Lear victoriously, and this time silently, but she began to treat him with a new caution, even smiling at him if their glances happened to meet during the quiet evenings— or at least drawing her lips back from her teeth.

And so Mother's Day arrived.

The dieffenbachia, identified as such by a visitor and watered and occasionally fed by Leslie (just as Isabel ministered to the birdbath), throve remorse-

lessly. By mid-July it appeared jungly enough to produce coconuts or bananas, but all it put forth was a
succession of new leaves, their pointed, needle-tight
furl of pale green emerging at the top one at a time.

The fresh growth seemed to require a living sacri-
fice at the bottom. Left to herself, Mrs. Lear would
have actively enjoyed the doomed and orange-
blotched droop of what had been so tough and indomi-
table a few days earlier, but Leslie or Isabel or Mrs.
Sedillo, who came twice a week to clean, always
nipped it off early. The parting of leaves and what
could only be called trunk was marked by a ladder
of whitish striations that looked like handholds for
baboons or worse.

The same visitor who had pronounced the plant
to be dieffenbachia was also obliging enough to tell
Mrs. Lear its other name as she was leaving: dumb
cane.

"Dumb cane?" repeated Mrs. Lear civilly. "With
a b?"

"That's right." The woman—tall, brisk, and knowledgeable—was something to do with the library
board. "It's poisonous, or at any rate it can cause the
tongue to swell enough to cause choking."

"Interesting," managed Mrs. Lear through a blur
of shock and rage. She closed the front door and in
a current of air the plant stirred its leaves mockingly.
"Fortunately, it doesn't look tempting enough to eat."

She retreated to her room. Hands fisted at her sides,
she paced the rose broadloom—seventy-eight, sev-
enty-nine, eighty—only pausing dangerously once at
the glass doors opening onto the patio. *Poison. Dumb*

cane. Leslie's private joke, relished a little more every time he dissolved vivid blue plant-food in water to feed the monstrous thing.

Kill it? Mrs. Lear had brought her golf clubs from the east; she needn't even go too close.

Or confront Leslie?

Neither. He and Isabel were going out to dinner tomorrow night.

They left the house at a quarter of six, but Mrs. Lear waited for the last red coal of a sunset to burn itself out before, properly equipped, she set forth on the mission which had been delayed by a procession of obstacles.

The sky was thick with stars, and after a moment or two on the lawn outside her bedroom she didn't need the flashlight. Forty feet of grass and then a band of stony ground and pinons brought her to the door of Leslie's workshop. Here, although the end drawer in the kitchen held a neatly tagged key, she used a hammer to smash all the glass out of the pane above the lock. She was meticulous about it, in spite of her acute sense of time, like someone parched but deliberately letting the water run cold from the finally reached faucet.

Inside, the wall switch was where her gloved hand expected to find it. She snapped the light on and took one greedy and comprehensive look before turning it off and activating the flashlight instead and placing it on a wheeled stool.

It was a big room, about thirty by fifteen, floored in concrete. Against one wall were stacks and piles of material, glass and plastic as well as wood in various thicknesses. Another wall, covered in pegboard, might have been transplanted intact from an expensive hardware store.

There was a couch, a sink, a tilt-topped desk, a long workbench with various tools clamped to it, something that might have been a lathe, a chest of the kind found in dentists' offices with at least a dozen shallow drawers.

The workbench was bolted to the floor, but Mrs. Lear inflicted a good deal of damage on it with both ends of the claw hammer. She hurled the chest drawers with their thousands of small compartmented metal objects, hearing wood shatter on impact, and while the noise of the rolling and settling contents still echoed she seized a sharp-pointed tool from the pegboard and ruptured tubes of paint and epoxy and other compounds.

She found nothing remotely identifiable in the flipped-through pages of the drawing pad on the desk, unless possibly what was either an old-fashioned clothespin or a primitive doll. Although her soul longed for a fire, even a small one, she contented herself with shredding the paper. She stoppered the sink and turned both faucets on full, and then she retrieved the flashlight, left the glassless door standing wide, and returned to the house.

According to her watch, which she removed at once, the whole trip had taken eight minutes. Mrs. Lear changed swiftly into nightgown, housecoat, and slippers, and called the police. She gave her name and Leslie's and the address, and said tensely that there was a prowler outside, almost certainly in an outbuilding, and would they send someone at once as she was alone here? Yes, all the doors *were* locked, but hurry!

The Gillises were punctilious about letting her know where they could be reached, and Mrs. Lear dialed that number next. To Leslie she ended up, "They know there's someone in the house, because the light went out as soon as I pulled back a curtain— so please get here as fast as you can!"

The two cars arrived almost together, the police marginally first. By that time, Mrs. Lear had scrubbed her face to a soapy shine and armed herself with one of her golf clubs, letting steaming hot water run into the tub and out again as she did so. As she had known she must, she told her story twice, first to the horrified Isabel, who insisted on getting them both a brandy, and then to the police and Leslie when they came back from their inspection of the ravaged workshop.

Except for the central action, the routine she described was so true of the many evenings when the Gillises were out that Mrs. Lear felt thoroughly natural with it: the television program watched for a while after her dinner, the retreat to her part of the house for an early bath—about eight-fifteen, she thought. She couldn't really describe the sound or sounds that had alerted her, because she hadn't actively been listening, but something had made her pull back folds of curtain from the patio door and a moving light in the direction of the workshop had been extinguished at once.

The police, for whom troublesome mothers-in-law

came equipped with broken bottles or blunter instruments, had already summed up her total pallor, her buffed nails in their natural polish, her snowily collared and cuffed navy housecoat. They made a dutiful note of the two youths who had come looking for yard work the week before, surprising Leslie in the act of filling a wheelbarrow with tumbleweeds that kept springing up among the gravel around the swimming pool, suggested a large dog or protective iron grillwork, and departed.

Mrs. Lear, whose tightly clutched forearms appeared to be containing a delayed reaction, was in fact hugging herself. Depression and loss were beginning to overtake Leslie visibly now that the immediate excitement had passed and there was no longer any male officialdom for whom to look vigorous and purposeful.

He suffered, she knew, from occasional insomnia. She rose from her chair, making a noticeable effort of it, and said in a mildly imploring tone they had never heard from her before, "Could you spare me one of your sleeping pills, Leslie? I really think—"

Thus brought to their senses, the Gillises apologized for having left her to face the night's unnerving incident alone. Isabel cosseted her into bed and brought her a glass of water from the bathroom, thereby being afforded a first-hand acquaintance with the still-wet tub, the lingeringly moist air, the damp towel slung from the rail.

Mrs. Lear even took the sleeping pill, although she felt as calm and luxuriously assuaged as if she had actually lain and been lapped about in warm water.

Dumb cane . . . The slate perhaps not wiped clean, but the balance at least somewhat redressed.

The next day went askew from the start.

Instead of leaving for his customary three hours at his office, Leslie elected to start repairing the havoc in the workshop. At ten, Isabel's Spanish teacher called; an ulcerated tooth forced her to cancel the afternoon class. Isabel, greeted with this news on her return from the mailbox, thought for a moment and said in that case, as there was no marketing that couldn't wait until tomorrow, she might as well spend the whole day in and give Leslie a hand with the workshop, poor lamb.

At ten thirty, determined not to engage in any propitiatory mother-in-law work, Mrs. Lear settled herself in the living room with a magazine. At ten thirty-five, she discovered that she did not like being alone with the marshaled array of great oval leaves across and a little down the room from her.

She tried to analyze the situation while pretending to concentrate on a formal interior done in saffron and oyster. The plant, surely in Leslie's confidence from the beginning, had had ample time to receive intelligence from the grass on which Mrs. Lear had walked and the pinons against which she had brushed on her way to the workshop last night; Isabel had opened the windows early after their unusual locking. But for all the hostility which it was exuding like a malign fragrance, it could not suddenly start to lurch at her, hitching itself in laborious half rounds. The rugs would bunch up and stop it.

Here, become aware of something slightly amiss in her thinking and intending to examine it, Mrs. Lear stood up sharply instead, letting the magazine hit the floor with a cracking sound, and took refuge in her room.

At noon, Isabel came back to the house to slice cold chicken for sandwiches. Although there was no retrieving the designs Leslie had unearthed and meant to go to work on with fresh ideas, they were actually getting somewhere.

Mrs. Lear, who had had to avert her face to conceal a little spasm of pleasure, watched her spread mayonnaise. "Does Leslie ever think up toys? It seems such a large field." Like most of her utterances of late, this one had been formulated in the quiet of her room, and although she could no longer tack down the exact association she was quite sure that she wanted to know the answer.

"Toys?" Isabel sprinkled salt and pepper, closed and deftly halved the sandwiches, slid them into a plastic bag. "He might, I only get to hear about his ideas when they've reached a certain stage . . . I think I'll bring some wine and try to fool us into thinking it's a picnic."

Mrs. Lear attempted to take her customary nap but could not. It was as if some jeering enemy had managed to get in and disarrange all the furniture of her mind, so that when she started down some calming path as a prelude to sleep she bumped into something that had no right to be there. *Dolls*, she thought, and threw back her coverlet.

Perhaps another of Leslie's pills. Isabel had had

the prescription refilled last week; he couldn't have reached the counting stage. Mrs. Lear put on a robe, opened her door, listened to the silence of the house, and proceeded very quietly to the Gillises' bedroom.

And she must have dropped off, if only for a few minutes, because at some point they had come in and put on their bathing suits. A side wing of one window stood wide, and although only a portion of curving concrete deck was visible Mrs. Lear could hear the faint slosh of disturbed water and, over it, Isabel saying, "—did discuss it very thoroughly before I called Mother, and we agreed that if she came it was to be for good. And now, just because this horrible business has cast a blight over everything—"

"It has nothing to do with the workshop." That was Leslie, temperate—and so, Mrs. Lear knew, with all the more staying power. "You don't realize it because it isn't directed at you, but your mother is getting extremely odd in the way she looks at me."

"Darling, you've been so angelic about all this that it's hard for you to see, but Mother's in a difficult position after all those years in her own house, wondering if she's really welcome. It takes time to—"

"It's been five months. And I'm not talking about any kind of fear, I'm talking about animosity. To put it mildly."

Mrs. Lear stood like something made of stone. After a few seconds of silence Isabel said, "Oh, really, Leslie. Why on earth? You must have some kind of theory if you're taking it all this seriously."

"All right, I think your mother was under a slight

misapprehension down in Puerto Vallarta just at the beginning. I think—"

Mrs. Lear took an uncontrollable step forward as the live wire of her hatred of Leslie Gillis came hissing and sparking free of the tangle in which it usually hid. Her indrawn breath was not of recognition but savage scorn; she lost a few words in the *How dare he?* that went ricocheting around in her head.

"But even granted a grain of truth there—" oh, clever! nothing disarmed like the appearance of concession! "—that was three years ago, darling, and I have to break it to you that to Mother men are a necessary evil. She had one, it's as simple as that. So—"

Leslie was fully as artful as Isabel—his "Then I don't know" sounded so wrung that she became coaxing at once.

"I'll tell you what, darling. I'll call Marietta. I think dinner would be best, even if I don't promise to accept her verdict—after all, she hasn't practiced for years. In the meantime, I'll have a little talk with Mother and you have a little talk with yourself, hm? I'm chilly, are you? Let's move into the sun . . ."

Even if their voices had not begun to fade, Mrs. Lear could have borne no more. What had the air of a partial yielding was only one of Isabel's temporizings, clothing a basic refusal, but how long would she hold out against Leslie's displeasure, how long see her settled happiness in jeopardy?

Not long.

Not really an asylum, they would say to their friends, but simply a very nice place where there was a professional staff to cope with people who had developed eccentricities. They had some patients there with Alzheimer's Disease, too. The gardens were lovely.

Mrs. Lear ground her teeth. Never.

She got through the rest of the afternoon, even helping Isabel in the kitchen, and dinner, remembering to pull her lips back at Leslie, although her future seemed to have taken on a quickened tempo. The unknown Marietta was a psychiatrist, of course. There was certainly nothing wrong with Mrs. Lear, but everybody knew that surgeons cut, editors edited, and psychiatrists found something badly askew. Naughty Marietta, thought Mrs. Lear in an instant's merriment.

Leslie went to bed early, pleading his labors in the workshop, although he had not been too tired after his coffee to wash the plant's hideous leaves. "It needs to breathe," he told Mrs. Lear for perhaps the tenth time, as if in the hope of her assuming this loving task, and she said ambiguously, "Does it?"

Isabel took a shower and returned in a thin drift of violet to read, as she often did when Leslie retired before ten. Tonight, however, she had a certain geared intensity which seemed to presage the "little talk." Mrs. Lear was by this time well prepared for it; she intended to be by turns astonished, hurt, and speculative. Was Isabel quite sure, she would ask, that this charge wasn't connected with Leslie's recently acquired habit of muttering to himself? Isabel hadn't heard him? Well, no doubt he made more effort when she was within earshot, but . . .

By its very nature, not talking to oneself would be difficult to prove. It would certainly muddy the issue.

The minutes went by and nothing happened except the arrival of a cool breeze through one of the open windows. At once the plant stirred tinily in its gratified, lamplit doze, and with the safeguarding presence of another person in the room Mrs. Lear, who of late had been unable to find a book that held her attention for more than two or three pages, lifted her head from the magazine abandoned that morning and stared at it boldly.

And closed her eyes in horror as her brain informed her as to what she saw, and opened them again to the same silently peeping atrocity.

He had frozen alertly, the tiny brown man who clung in the V between trunk and one of the arching stems, overlaid by a shorter curving horn that fed the leaves. Everything about him said that he was a savage, no more than six or seven inches tall but so perfectly to scale that if his dreadful host were allowed to achieve its true proportions he would be life-sized.

Leslie brought him food, obviously, while appearing only to tend the plant. And instructions, which he was preparing to carry out tonight.

No, sooner than that. Now.

He rippled alertly when Mrs. Lear got "Isabel!" out of a convulsed throat. What, inquired an answering tautness in her chest, if he should come swarming down the trunk and make for her chair? But of course he did not; with the cunning of all his species he became as innocent as lamplight and chlorophyll.

Isabel didn't need a further summons. She got up at once and crossed the room, bending as compelled by the wild strength of the grip on her wrist. Mrs. Lear's broken whispering was scarcely more than a brushing against the spellbound silence. "Look, in the plant, in the middle, a third of the way up—he isn't a doll, he's a little man, he's alive, he's *alive*—"

"Yes, I see him," Isabel whispered back after moments. She had gone very white, but her control as she assisted her mother up and out of the chair was almost absolute. "See, there's your golf club." She turned Mrs. Lear gently toward the corner where the iron still stood, forgotten memento of the night before. "Can you hold that and keep watch while I call—"

"*Not Leslie!*"

"No, no, the—police. I think they should know about this. Keep the club behind your back, so as not to provoke him. Can you do that, Mother? I'll be right back."

Isabel did not pause at the near telephone extension just inside the dining room, but, out from under Mrs. Lear's eye, ran to the bedroom, snapped the light on ruthlessly, and shook Leslie awake—with some difficulty because in spite of his physical fatigue he had taken one of his sleeping capsules. "Leslie, *Leslie*, you've got to get up this instant! Oh, darling, you were so right about Mother. She's in the living room, obviously back in childhood, frantic about a favorite doll she calls her little man. She's convinced it's hidden in the plant, so you'll just have to keep promising to get it for her while I call Dr. Fellowes. This is way beyond Marietta—"

"Good God. Her little man," repeated Leslie, anchoring in his barely cleared head a phrase totally alien in connection with his mother-in-law, and made tidying gestures at his pajamas as he headed for the closet.

Isabel snatched up the receiver in a display of panic that sent him out the door. "There isn't *time* for a robe!"

Because how long could hallucination be counted on to last, even bolstered by her pretense that she had seen it, too? And the acute paranoia which was essential to this long-awaited moment?

That people crossed Mrs. Lear at their peril had been a fact of Isabel's life as far back as she could remember. That to an informed eye Mrs. Lear had shown signs of increased instability the Thanksgiving before last was more or less to be expected. The two circumstances had not come together for Isabel until she fell blazingly in love for the first time in her life, knew that a snatched meeting once a week under the guise of a Spanish class was not enough, and realized that nothing would induce Leslie to let her go. And realized, too, that a divorce action brought by her and fought every step of the way by Leslie would be costly as well as interminable.

Why should she wait all that time, and part with all that admittedly attractive money—Isabel was thirty-nine, and the man in question five years younger—when there was Mother of the implacable grudges, the powerful wrists conditioned by years of golf, the thought processes as burrowing as the work of moles?

But in spite of her determination and her months of tightrope-walking, her orchestration of Mrs. Lear's venom wherever possible—the oblique pointing out of the ugly plant to Leslie had certainly borne fruit— and her triumph and sense of imminence at last night's rampage in the workshop, Isabel was not without sensibility. Leslie had had time to reach the living room, perhaps even now—he would be speaking quietly—was promising to hand over the object of terror.

She had been contemplating the mirrored eyes it was impossible to imagine as one day being a bleached and stony lavender. Very delicately, she closed the bedroom door.

The Old Barn on the Pond

He came back on a raw, darkly glistening day in March, but it was not at all the triumphant return he had planned. It was a hasty, off-balance thing, like being pushed rudely onto a stage before the raised trumpets had blown a single note.

Conlon's letter—the letter that had brought him tumbling up from New York to this inhospitable part of the New England countryside—was still in his pocket. He had never liked Conlon, but the architect was Marian's cousin and it would have looked odd, when he had the old barn remodeled, to have given the job to someone else. And now here was Conlon writing ". . . have been approached by friends about the possibility of renting your property here for the summer, with an option to buy. As they have a young child, they would like to drain the pond, and although I told them I was certain you would not permit this—"

For a moment the typed lines had blurred before Howard Hildreth's eyes—except for that one staring phrase.

Drain the pond.

"Not yet," he thought lucidly—"not after only six

months." Anonymous in the Forty-second Street Library, he had read up on the subject, and learned that under certain conditions—depth of water, amount of rainfall, and other climatic factors—this kind of soil might have sucked its secret under at the end of a year, provided there was no extensive digging.

But not yet. He had sat down at once to write a brief note of refusal, but another phrase struck up at him from Conlon's letter. ". . . I was certain you would not permit this—"

A deliberate challenge? Bill Conlon was Marian's cousin, remember, and had been away at the time. Better go up there, stay a week or two, establish the impression of keeping the place as a country retreat upon which he might descend at any time. It was only necessary for Conlon; the townspeople, he was sure, accepted his remodeling of the barn as proof of his faith that his missing wife would some day return.

At that thought, alone in his comfortable apartment, Howard Hildreth shuddered . . .

On the station platform there were gratifying little whispers and stirs of recognition—"Isn't that Howard Hildreth, the playwright? I'm sure it is"—and a turning of heads which he pretended not to see. He could hardly pretend not to see Conlon, striding across the platform toward him with his fair head a little cocked. Conlon had Marian's eyes, light gray with a peculiar curl of lid; but that was the only physical resemblance between them.

Hildreth put out a hand and said with an air of geniality, "Well, this is kind. I hope you haven't been meeting trains all day?"

Conlon sent one of his roving glances around the platform. "Matter of fact, a fellow in our office was supposed to catch this one but he seems to have missed it. Come on, I'll give you a lift."

After his first annoyance at Conlon's balloon-pricking, Hildreth was pleased; this would give him a chance to demonstrate his calm. He said as they got into the car, "I can see how you thought I wouldn't be using the place this summer. I'd have been in touch with you sooner about coming up but we've had a little trouble in the cast."

He waited for Conlon to show interest, but the other man only said, "Too bad. Play still going well?"

"Very, thanks."

"I particularly liked"—Conlon turned a sharp corner with care—"the third act. It packs quite a wallop. Are you working on a new play?"

"I am, as a matter of fact, and I thought a little peace and quiet . . . You know New York," said Hildreth resignedly. In his tone were autograph hunters, sheaves of fan mail, a telephone carrying an invitation with each ring.

And part of it was true. *The Far Cry* was that rarest of things, a hit first play, and the playbill's revelation that it had been eight years in the writing had given an additional fillip. Eight years—what constancy! No wonder that superb third act expertly shivered like a diamond. Here was no glib young creature with a gift for bubbling out dialogue but a major talent who cut his work like a precious stone.

So the critics said, and the important hostesses, and Howard Hildreth, who had been laughed at in this little town, and had his credit refused and his electric light turned off, found his champagne all the winier and forgot those few hours of frantic typing . . .

". . . not a word," Conlon was saying, and Hildreth wrenched his attention from his play, his other self. They were out of the town now, rising into little hills and woodland, puddled and glinted yellowly by a sky which, having rained earlier, was now gloating over it.

Hildreth's mind spun back and recaptured the sense of his companion's words. He said, "Nor I. But I refuse to believe . . . you knew Marian—"

"I think she's dead," said Conlon bluntly without turning his head. "I think she was dead all the time the police were out looking for her."

"But . . . where—?" said Hildreth in a shocked voice.

Conlon waved a hand at the dimming landscape. "There's almost as much water as there is land around here," he said. "Lake, marshes, even quicksand. She had such a horror of things eaten up in the water, remember?"

"Stop!" said Hildreth with genuine violence. "You mustn't talk about her as though—Besides, Marian was happy, she would never have—"

"Committed suicide, or disappeared on purpose?" said Conlon when it was apparent that Hildreth was not going to finish. "Oh, I never thought she had. As you say, I knew Marian . . . here we are."

The car had descended a gentle twisting curve. At the bottom, opposite a stand of birches and set perhaps a hundred feet in from the road, was the pond, as round and clear as a wondering eye, lashed by willows that looked lamplit in the approaching dusk.

On the far side of it, on a slight rise, stood the creamy new structure, the remodeled barn, which six months ago had been weather-beaten planks and a wobbly brown-painted door. There was no breath of wind; the house and reflection met themselves in a mirror stillness.

Howard Hildreth gazed, and his heart raced with such horror that he wondered if he was about to have a stroke. He wrenched at his horn-rimmed glasses with a trembling hand, and heard Conlon say curiously, "Are you all right, Howard?"

"Yes. These damned glasses—the doctor warned me that I needed new ones." Even the effort of speaking calmly seemed to put a nutcracker pressure on his heart. "You've done a beautiful job of remodeling the barn, Bill. The photographs you sent didn't do it justice. Shall we go on in?"

The drive up to the house itself was screened by willows. By the time Conlon had helped him inside with his bags, Hildreth was able to say almost normally, "Well, here we are. You'll have a drink, won't you?"

Conlon shook his head. He said with a hand on the doorknob, "Sarah—Sarah Wilde, you know—ordered a few essentials for the kitchen, so you ought to get through the night without starving. Well—"

Hildreth did not press him to stay. He said, standing in the open doorway, "These friends of yours that I had to disappoint—do I know them? What's their name?"

"Pocock," said Conlon promptly, and it was so unlikely a name that Hildreth had to believe him. Or was it meant to be a shortened version of poppycock?

He did not even look around at the long studio that took up most of the lower front of the house. He waited tensely for the final retreat of Conlon's motor, and when even the echoes were gone he opened the door and walked the length of the driveway in the lonely frog-sounding dusk.

And there was light enough—just enough—to show him the same sickening apparition. On the far side of the pond stood the new barn, radiantly pale, bearing no resemblance to its former weather-beaten brown. But at his feet, glassily etched on the surface of the water, lay the old barn, with its knotholes and weather stains and the wide brown-painted door.

Hildreth drew a long uneven breath. There was no one to see him step squashily to the reed-grown edge of the pond and dip a hand in the icy water. The old barn quaked under the willows, and shook and was presently still again—but it was still the old barn . . .

He did not drink—Marian had—but he took a tranquilizer and headed for his reviews like a child to its mother's skirts. The *Times, Tribune, Daily News,* the out-of-town papers. "Last night at the Odeon Theatre this critic was refreshingly jolted . . ."

"*The Far Cry* is just that in a season so far noted for its weary offerings . . ." "Let us hope we do not have to wait another eight years for the next Hildreth play . . ."

And presently he knew what had happened to him out there at the pond's edge. Autosuggestion, hallucination—at any rate, there was an accepted term for it; if beauty lay in the beholder's eye, so did other things. He knew what was under that pleasant and pastoral surface, and at the subconscious tension of his mind, because Conlon had been with him, his retina had produced the appropriate setting.

But not for Conlon, with all his suspicions—and in retrospect, the man had exuded suspicion. Conlon had looked at the pond and seen nothing amiss; for him, the still water had reflected only his personal creation of shored-up beams and plaster and creamy paint and whatever else went into his remodeling of an old structure. The thought gave Hildreth a satisfaction that, keyed up as he was, bordered on triumph.

What a joke on them all, he mused as he broiled the steak Sarah Wilde had left in the refrigerator, if only he, Hildreth, could see this watery witness, gaze at it in their presence, say casually, "Lovely day, isn't it?"—and stand there calmly and casually in the midst of their blindness.

Not that the reflection would be on the pond in the morning. Tonight it had simply been a product of nerves and fatigue, and a good night's sleep would erase it. Still, he was shaken, and he prudently avoided his after-dinner coffee. He darkened the downstairs, flipped on the staircase switch, and went up to his bedroom.

And came face to face with a portrait of Marian which he never knew had been taken.

As the blood came and went from his heart more slowly, he realized that the matted and mounted photograph on the bureau was not a portrait but an enlarged snapshot; on closer inspection it bore a telltale grain and blurriness. It was in color and it showed Marian laughing. There was a halo of sunlight on the close curls that scrambled over her beautifully shaped head, and the same light picked out the comma of mirth beside her mouth although her short, soft, full white throat was in shadow.

Marian laughing . . .

. . . laughing at his play, which she was not supposed to have seen at all until he had written the final word—*Curtain*. Managing to say through the laughter, "My dear playwright, you don't mean to say you've been muddling around with this thing for eight years and missed the whole *point?* It ought to be satire at the end, don't you see, and you fox the audience in the third act instead of this heavy Russian gloom going on and on? It would have such a wonderful, final crack-the-whip effect, and you could get rid of Anna coming in and saying"—she draggled at her hair, which was much too short and curly for draggling—"whatever that long lugubrious speech is."

Her face was brilliant with excited laughter. "Oh, *wait* till I tell Bill and Sarah we've found a way to finish the Odyssey at last! They'll be so—Howard, for heaven's sake, I'm only—*Howar*—"

For such a full throat, it was as soft and weak as a child's . . .

In the morning Hildreth looked at the pond, and the old weather-beaten barn was still there, shaken and distorted under a gently falling rain. Disturbingly, he was not terrified or shocked or even very surprised; it was as though, at some point during his sleep, his brain had accepted this phenomenon as readily as the pond had accepted Marian.

After breakfast he made arrangements for renting a car, and then he called Sarah Wilde.

It was through Sarah, who also had an apartment in the building on East Tenth Street, that he had met Marian Guest. Sarah and Marian were copywriters in the same advertising agency, and although Hildreth had a sober loathing of advertising copy and all the people who wrote it—there was a flippancy about them that appalled him—Sarah was well connected. An aunt of hers was a best-selling novelist, and it had never harmed any hopeful playwright to have even a hearsay acquaintance with a publisher. He had cultivated Sarah in the elevator, lent her an umbrella one day, and ultimately wound up at a party in her apartment.

And there was Marian, sitting on the floor although there were chairs available. She wore black slacks and an expensive-looking white silk shirt with a safety pin where a button should have been, and, profile tilted in the lamplight, she was explaining with zest how she had come by her black eye and scraped cheekbone. She had been walking her dog George and had fallen over a sheep on a leash. "The man said it was a Bedlington but he was obviously trying to cover up his own confusion. Poor George bit him, not the man, and I think he's got a hair ball."

Although there were two or three other girls present, all with a just-unboxed Madison Avenue attractiveness, the attention seemed to cluster about Marian. She said presently to Howard Hildreth in her boyish and uninhibited voice, "You look terribly broody. What are you hatching?"

"A play," he told her distantly, and it might have been the very distance that attracted her, as it was the attention focused on her that attracted him. At any rate, he ended up taking her home to her apartment on Barrow Street, drinking innumerable cups of black coffee, and telling her about his play. He began challengingly, prepared for amusement when she learned that he had already been working on it for three years; but she listened, her light clear eyes as wide and sober as a child's.

She said, "What do you do—for an income, I mean?"

When he said flatly, "I'm a shoe clerk," she stared past him with a kind of wondering sadness.

"How marvelous," she had said, "to give that much of a damn about anything."

There was Marian, summed up in a single sentence; even after they were married she never told him anything as self-revelatory as that. And under the influence of her respect for his dedication, his work, which had always been his Work to him, was able to come out in the open with its capital letter. Until she had defected—

But Hildreth had learned to discipline his mind, and he did it now.

He said into the telephone, "Sarah? I'm an ingrate for not calling you last night to tell you how much I like the way you've done the place—as well as providing my dinner—but . . ."

Sarah Wilde cut him off easily. "Do you like it? I'm glad. It's rather a lot of lavender, but you did specify—"

"Yes," Hildreth gazed, secretly entertained, at the lavender draperies, the lavender cushions, round and square and triangular, piled on the black tweed couch. Lavender—Marian's favorite color. Any doubters close to Marian could not help saying to themselves, "Well, if he can live with that . . ."

"It's very soothing," he said to Sarah with the defensive air of a husband standing up for his wife's vagaries. "Very restful. I like the picture on my bureau, by the way."

It was as though the telephone cord had been pulled taut between them. "It is a good one, isn't it? I took it—oh, some time last summer, I think, and I'd forgotten all about it until Bill Conlon happened to see it and thought you'd like an enlargement."

"It was very thoughtful of you both," said Hildreth with perfect evenness. "That's the way I think of her, you know. Laughing. I suppose Bill's told you that I haven't given up hope."

"Of course you haven't," said Sarah, bright and artificial.

Between them, in the small silence that followed, lay the many trips that he and Conlon had taken to view unidentified female bodies which corresponded even roughly with Marian's age and height. It was grim work, which helped; he was always a thoroughly pale and shaken man. And with each fruitless trip, because of the very nature of such an errand, the official belief that Marian Hildreth was dead had grown. Hildreth could tell that Sarah believed it too—in which, of course, she was quite right.

She was veering quickly away from the subject now, saying something about dinner this week. Hildreth accepted for Thursday evening, adding with a deprecating little laugh that he trusted it wouldn't be an Occasion; he'd come up here to get started on his new play.

"No, just two or three people," Sarah assured him. "I did tell you, didn't I, how much I liked *The Far Cry?* I thought I knew what was coming in the third act, but it was one time I loved being made a fool of."

Hildreth thanked her, a trifle aloofly, and there was not the smallest alarm along his nerves. He suspected that Sarah and Conlon, mere acquaintances six months ago, would be married before the year was out, but the fact that they had undoubtedly seen the play together didn't matter. They could not say, "That last act sounds like Marian," because as far as they knew Marian had never laid eyes on the script—she had said wryly, in fact, two or three days before that last night, "Howard thinks I'll mark his baby, like a gypsy . . ."

(What a very tellable joke it would have been, what an irresistible nugget for gossip columns, because Marian's was not a secret-keeping nature: that Howard Hildreth had toiled unremittingly over his play for eight years, and in the space of a single hour his wife, who had never written anything but tongue-in-cheek praise of vinyl tile and slide fasteners, had offhandedly supplied the satirical twist that made it a success.)

Even at the thought Hildreth felt a qualm of nausea. Although his portable typewriter stood ready on the desk at the far end of the studio, with a fresh ream of yellow paper beside it, he let himself out the front door into the falling rain and walked to the pond's edge. There was the old barn, shaking dimly under the falling drops, and he knew that in some terrible way he was drawing strength from this private vision, locked under the willows for his eyes, and apparently for his alone . . .

A notion of incipient madness slid across his mind, but he looked quickly about him and everything else was sane and clear. If Marian thought to retaliate after death . . .

He drew himself up sharply.

In the afternoon he was gracious to the editor of the local newspaper, with the result that his favorite publicity picture appeared in the next morning's issue. He was holding his horn-rimmed glasses with one earpiece casually collapsed, and the three-quarter turn of his head almost concealed the double chin developed since those lean days.

". . . seeking inspiration for his new play," said the account below, proudly, and, "Residents will recall the still-unresolved disappearance of Mrs. Marian

Hildreth six months ago. Mrs. Hildreth, 38, told her husband late on the evening of October 4, 1963, that she was going out for a walk. She did not return, and no trace of her has since been found. Mr. Hildreth maintains his staunch belief that his wife is still alive, possibly suffering from a loss of memory . . ."

Hildreth read with calm pleasure the rest of the telling—how the pond on the property had been dragged without result. The police had indeed dragged it over his demurs—"Oh, come now, she wouldn't fall into a pond she's lived beside for five years"— and then came the heavily tactful, "Mr. Hildreth, your wife wasn't—er . . . ?"

Because Marian's more madcap exploits were not unknown to the local police. They viewed her with a tolerant and even an indulgent eye—that was the effect she had on people; but under the circumstances they could not rule out a tragic and alcoholic whim.

"No," Hildreth had said with transparent stoutness. "Oh, she may have had a highball or two after dinner . . ."

He knew, he had known at the moment of her death, that the marital partner was usually Suspect Number One. But that had not actually held true in little Ixton, Connecticut. If there had been any whisper of discord, any suggestion of dalliance by either party, any prospect of inheriting money—or even if Marian's life had been insured—the police might have looked deeper than they did. As it was, they walked past the burlaped yew, the burlaped roses, Marian's burlaped body, and then announced that they would drag the pond.

This procedure netted them two ancient inner tubes, a rotted and hinged object which had once been the hood of a convertible, and a rust-fretted oil drum which seemed to have spawned a great many beer cans. If the police had returned at just after dark, when one particular piece of burlap among the yews had been lifted free of its stiffened secret, and the secret transferred to the now officially blameless water . . . but, predictably, they had not.

They could have no further reason for dragging the pond now—indeed, thought Hildreth, they would need a warrant. And for a warrant they would need evidence.

That was the safety element in a spur-of-the-moment murder. The cleverest planners—Hildreth rejected the word *killers*—had come to grief over elaborate timetables, unsuspected correspondence, a hint of fear dropped somewhere. There could be none of that in this case. Neither he nor Marian had known what was coming until that moment of her crowing laughter, that intolerable tearing-down of the secrecy and seriousness of his Work.

It was not so much that Marian had burst the bonds of curiosity and somehow contrived to unlock the desk drawer which housed his script, nor even that she had slipped at least temporarily into the ranks of the people who found him clownishly amusing. It was that she was right. Like someone engaged on a painstaking tapestry, he had been following stitch after stitch and lost sight of the pattern, which had leaped at once to Marian's unbothered and mischievous eye.

It was as if . . . he could not say at the time, because his logic had smoked away like cellophane in a flame. Later, more calmly, he could compare himself to a woman who, after a long and difficult labor, watches the doctor merrily bearing the infant off to his own home.

But there was no evidence, and he would not be tricked or trapped. His visit here—the first since the five weeks or so after he had reported Marian missing—would proclaim his innocence. Not to the police—he wasn't worried about them—but to Bill Conlon and Sarah Wilde, the only people who, close to Marian, might just possibly . . .

Hildreth arranged yellow paper beside his uncovered typewriter in the white-walled lavender-and-black studio, but he did not, that morning or the next or the one after that, commence even the roughest work on a new play.

He told himself defensively that he had spent several months under considerable strain; a man didn't bounce back from that right away. And critical success was paralyzing in itself: there was the inevitable restudying of the first work in search of the magic ingredient, and the equally inevitable fear of comparison with a second.

At no time did he allow it to cross his mind that there were one-play playwrights as there were one-book novelists, and that his one play would still be in various stages of rewriting except for Marian's unruly wit. But there was a moment when, seated blankly at the typewriter, he thought, *Do I look like the pond?* and got up and crossed the room to examine himself in a mirror.

But no; he hadn't changed at all in spite of his damp little tremor of fright. And if he could see the truth on the pond's surface, surely he could see it on his own? There was the gained weight, granted, but his dark eyes gave back their old serious look, his eyebrows were forbiddingly level, a lock of hair—now pampered by his New York barber—still hung with dedication.

But when he stared long enough and hard enough, moving his face to within an inch or two of the mirror, tiny little Howard Hildreths peeked out of the pupils, and behind them—

Ah, behind *them* . . .

He developed a kind of triumphant passion for the pond. He watched it ballooned with clouds, or covered with nervous little wrinkles under a sudden wind. He saw the weather-beaten planks and the brown door warp and fly to pieces under the miniature tidal waves caused by water bugs or perhaps frogs. Pretending to enjoy a cigarette in the course of a stroll, he took note of the passing cars that slowed for an admiring view of the clean creamy little house behind the willowed pond, and no car jerked to a shocked halt, no one screamed.

Hildreth had a Polaroid camera, and one afternoon, in a fascinated test, he took a picture of the pond. Conlon's photographs had shown no abnormality, but this time it was he who was pressing the shutter. The day warranted color film—the willows dripped and candled about the round eye of water, enameled so perfectly that it might have been a brooch.

Wouldn't it be odd, thought Hildreth, counting excitedly to sixty, if only the camera and I—?

He was peeling the paper shield away when Sarah Wilde's voice said at his shoulder, "Oh, may I see?"

The print and its fluttering attachment dropped to the ground.

Hildreth got only a swinging glimpse of Sarah's slanted white cheek, caught only the beginning of the rueful, "I'm sorry, I didn't mean—" before he bent, barely circumventing her; if necessary he would have put his shoe on the print.

As it was, he snatched it up and turned away, manufacturing a cough, while he finished stripping the shield. He said a second later, turning back, "Not bad, is it?" and handed the innocent color print to Sarah. No, not the camera and himself—only himself.

Sarah, he thought watchfully, was a remarkably beautiful young woman. Her dropped lashes were a thick unretouched silver-brown, her polished hair a slightly deeper brown; her gaze, when she lifted it, would be gray. With the suave red lipstick to counterpoint the water-color effect, she was quietly startling in any gathering.

"Very good indeed," she said, handing the print back by its edges. "The pond's so pretty, isn't it? Especially now."

She glanced at the circle of water and then back at Hildreth, who following her gaze had still seen the placidly mirrored old barn. A tremble of nerves ran along his throat. To control a wild impulse toward laughter he said in a considering, landownerish way,

"It seems quite full, but you've had heavy rains this month, haven't you?" and he slid the print casually into his coat pocket.

"Yes, it is full," said Sarah in her own considering tone, and there was no doubt about it; the eyes that moved from the pond to his face held some kind of—doubt? Challenge? Hildreth said coolly, "Well, if you'll excuse me, it's back to the typewriter," and he took a step away.

"Wait, I almost forgot what I came for." Sarah was dipping into her calf handbag. "Here—the mailman put this in my box instead of yours. Wonderful to get fan mail. Don't forget about dinner tonight—cocktails at six thirty."

It wasn't fan mail which Hildreth opened when the red Volkswagen had disappeared over the hill, but one of the many letters which, the police had told him, always arrived in the wake of a disappearance. This one was from "Someone Who Can Help," and in exchange for two hundred dollars mailed to an enclosed box number in Vermont the writer would put him in touch with his missing wife.

The maddening part of these communications was that they could not be ignored—at least, not by a man in whom hope supposedly sprang eternal. Hildreth, sitting down to write the form reply that thanked the writer and said he was turning the letter over to the officers in charge of the investigation, thought angrily that there ought to be a law.

The afternoon passed slowly. Conlon telephoned to say that there would be a plumber coming over to do something to the downstairs bath, and Hildreth said pettishly, "Really, Bill, forgive me, but I thought all that had been taken care of. One doesn't greet plumbers in the middle of Scene One, you know."

He was mollified a little later by a delegation from the local high-school magazine, asking humbly for a "Best Wishes from Howard Hildreth" to be photostated for the graduation issue. One of the shiny-haired, wide-eyed girls ventured close to his typewriter, in which Hildreth foresightedly kept a typed yellow sheet—the opening scene of *The Far Cry*—and he said at once, austerely, "Please don't—I have a 'thing' about work in progress."

It only added to their awe. But he had had it, thought Hildreth, presently seeing them to the door; he had had all the local adulation he wanted. Imperiously buying delicacies at the only market that carried them, he had seen the fawning face of the manager who only a year ago had told him that if his bill wasn't settled promptly he would find himself in the small-claims court.

He had been pointed out respectfully on the main street, and had declined invitations from the town's reigning hostess. More importantly, he had been accepted everywhere without a trace of suspicion; if there was any sentiment in the air, it was one of embarrassed pity for a man who so courageously continued to hope.

In a day or two he could go back to New York, having established to Bill Conlon and Sarah Wilde and everybody else that there was no question of his selling or even renting the property with its pretty, deadly pond.

He was all the more shocked, in the midst of these comfortable reflections, when at a little after three he had a call from a Sergeant Fisk at the police station. Some little girls looking for pussy willows in a field on the outskirts of the town had discovered a woman's leather handbag and part of a dress with some suggestive stains; would Hildreth please come down and see if he could identify them?

"Certainly," said Hildreth, staring angrily out the window. "Of course, being out in the weather, I imagine they're pretty well—?"

"No, sir, they were stuffed in the remains of an old stone wall and they're still in fair condition. Recognizable, anyway."

"I'll leave right away," said Hildreth, tempering his eagerness with the right amount of dread.

At the police station he was asked to wait—Sergeant Fisk would be right with him.

By four o'clock Sergeant Fisk still was not with him; at four thirty, fuming, Hildreth walked up to the uniformed man at the switchboard and said sharply, "I came here at the request of Sergeant Fisk to look at some objects for identification, and I cannot wait any longer. Please leave a message—"

"Just a minute, sir," said the policeman unruffledly, and slipped a plug into its socket and inquired for Sergeant Fisk. "There's a Mr. Hildreth here, been waiting since—okay, I'll tell him to go right in."

But the handbag and dress fragment, when Hildreth reached Sergeant Fisk's office, had been transferred to Lieutenant Martin's office, where there was some question as to their possible connection with the vanishing of a Colorado couple making a cross-country tour four months ago. Hildreth contained his temper as he went with the sergeant to Martin's office; he was, he remembered, a man who would do anything to find a clue to his wife's fate.

He was badly tempted when, at after five o'clock, he surveyed a rotted and mildewed navy calf handbag, empty, and the sleeve and half the bodice of what had once been a yellow wool dress. Why not say, "Yes, they're my wife's," and bury his face in his hands and be done with it?

Because, he thought with a feeling of having stepped back from the edge of a cliff, Marian had never worn yellow—she said it made her look like a two-legged hangover; and there was a suggestion of something on the leather lining of the bag that could easily be a nearly obliterated name or monogram. Hildreth had read what modern police laboratories could do with things like that. So he shook his head and said, "They're not my wife's," and with a shudder at the stains on the rotting yellow wool, "Thank God."

Three hours, he thought as he drove home seething in the rainy dusk; three hours on a fool's errand which he could not have risked refusing. Just barely time to dress for dinner at Sarah Wilde's—and then get out of here, tomorrow.

He was restored at the thought, and at the glimpse of the old barn quivering on the pond in the last of the light as he drove to Sarah's. His temper was further improved by Sarah's big, casually gay living room—two rooms thrown together in a very old salt-box—and the contrast between an open fire and a cold rattling rain on the windows.

The other guests were already established with drinks—Conlon, a Mr. and Mrs. Slater, and Mrs. Slater's decorative visiting sister.

Hildreth thawed, physically and temperamentally. He felt a slight jar of recognition when he was introduced to the Slaters, but he had undoubtedly encountered them on the station platform at some forgotten time, or in a local store. He noted with approval that Sarah had obviously got someone in for the evening, because there were sounds of kitchen activity while Sarah sat on the couch, in black and pearls, beside Conlon.

On the rare occasions when he and Marian had entertained, Marian had charged in and out like a demented puppy, crying, "My God, who's been watching the beans? Nobody!" Or, abashedly, "We all like nutmeg instead of pepper in our mashed potatoes, don't we?"

Sarah had turned her head and was gazing at him; somebody had clearly asked a question. Hildreth used a handkerchief on his suddenly damp forehead and temples and said, "I got wetter than I thought—that's really quite a downpour," and he got up to stand by the fire.

And the bad moment was gone, further wiped out by Sarah's "You said you mightn't be here long on this visit, Howard, so we're having your favorite dinner—you know, what you won't eat in restaurants."

"Don't tell me . . . ?" said Hildreth, delighted, but it was: trout, a crisp deep-gold outside, succulent white within, delicately enhanced by herbs that only hinted at themselves. He ate with deliberate pleasure, not succumbing until close to the end of dinner to his habit of providing backgrounds for people.

The extraordinarily good-looking sister from New Haven—her name was Vivian Hughes—seemed the kind of young woman who, convinced in her teens that she could have any man she wanted, had ended up with none; there was a kind of forced grace to the frequent turn of her head, and lines of discontent around her really striking green eyes.

Mrs. Slater wasn't a fair test, because she had ticketed herself earlier by a reference to the young twins they had left with a babysitter, and by her very casualness she had given herself away. She was the new and on the whole the best breed of mother, thought Hildreth approvingly; slender, amiable, intelligent, she kept her maternal dotings strictly for hearth and home.

Slater? Hildreth gazed obliquely through candlelight at the other man, perhaps a year or two younger than his own forty. The lean, polished, ruddy face suggested an outdoorsman, but everything else pointed to an executive. He went on gazing, and like an exposed print washed gently back and forth in developer, outlines began to emerge.

A desk, not executive grain, but scarred oak. Two telephones on it. A uniformed man in a far doorway saying, "Yes, sir, right away," then disappearing down one of a warren of corridors.

Yes, Slater was a police officer of some sort, or a detective, glimpsed or perhaps even talked to in the first stages of the investigation six months ago. And Sarah and Conlon hoped that he would be terrified by this recognition, and go to pieces. That was the whole point of this friendly little gathering.

How very disappointed they must be. Hildreth stirred his coffee tranquilly, because no motive for murder had existed until sixty seconds before Marian died, and there wasn't a single clue. In an enjoyment of the attention he now knew to be trained on him he said in a well-fed voice, "Marvelous dinner, Sarah. I don't know when I've had trout like that," and Sarah said, "As a matter of fact, you never have."

She was leaning forward a little in the candlelight, her gaze cool and removed. "The trout were from your pond, Howard, and they were caught this afternoon while you were down at the police station. You didn't know that Marian had had the pond stocked for you, as a birthday present, just before she—disappeared, because you love trout but never trust it in restaurants. We didn't know about it either until the friend who did it for her stopped by to see Bill a couple of weeks ago."

Hildreth's neck felt caught in one of those high white collars you saw on injured people; he could not turn it even when he heard Conlon's, "Nice fat trout, I thought, but lazy. They bit at anything."

. . . while he had sat in the police station, decoyed there by a telephone call.

"You all ate it," said Hildreth triumphantly, in a candlelight that had begun to tremble and dampen his face. "You all—"

"No. Ours was perch from the Old Town Fish Market," said Sarah, and although she continued to hold his gaze, her forehead had a cold glimmer and her mouth seemed clenched against a scream.

Hildreth lost them all then. He dropped his eyes, but instead of his dessert cup he saw his dinner plate, with the neat spiny bones from which all the succulent white flesh had been forked away. Marian's soft white throat, and the busy, inquisitive, nibbling mouths at the bottom of the pond, and the plump things placed on his plate—

He heard his chair go crashing back, and the gagging cry of horror that issued from his own throat as he plunged blindly for somewhere to be sick; and, from a mist, Slater's voice saying, ". . . looks like it. Very definitely. We'll get at it first thing in the morning . . ."

Good Neighbor

Mrs. GLASS advanced on the house across the road with the measureless aplomb of a woman who has been mastering Cub Scouts, school committees, and minor civic officials for years.

It was a small old house, adobe, settled under cottonwood trees as naturally as a toadstool and, in Mrs. Glass's opinion, as unhealthily. She noted with a kind of grim satisfaction that the arch-topped front door, weathered to the color of driftwood, had neither knocker nor bell.

Well, that was symbolic. These neglected old people shrank into the shell of their own hurt, and sometimes, even for Mrs. Glass, who had worked with Senior Citizens, it was very hard to get them out.

She used her knuckles on the door, smartly, and turned to contemplate her own domain across the way.

Gas lanterns, flickering invisibly in the morning sunlight, flanked a wide crushed-stone drive with its antiqued-wood sign: Griffin Acres. They were quarter acres, really, but beautifully landscaped around the expensive brand-new homes. This was no warren of a development; the houses—some trimmed with redwood, others with stone—faced each other at tactful angles.

Mrs. Glass's was the first on the right as you drove in. When the flaming-orange gas tank in the distance was repainted a soft green—as the developers had promised—you would hardly know it was there. Mrs. Glass gazed and marveled; it was difficult to believe that only six months ago Griffin Acres had been trees and fields and cawing crows.

She turned back to the door and had just lifted her hand to rap again when it opened. A small elderly woman with piled white hair and penetrating hazel eyes—the eyes of a girl, almost—said instantly, "I don't use cosmetics, as you see, and I never read magazines. I say this," the white head tipped disarmingly, "so as not to waste your time or mine."

Mrs. Glass took a moment to comprehend; then, as the door began a courteous waver in her direction, she laughed cheerfully. "Oh, *I* see. You are Mrs. Corey? I'm Stella Glass, your neighbor across the way, and I'm not selling a thing. I just came over to say hello."

Fleetingly, Mrs. Corey appeared to think that this had been accomplished, but then she widened the door again and said politely, "It's very kind of you. Won't you come in, Mrs. Glass?"

Mrs. Glass went in. She was consumed with curiosity about this poor old soul whom nobody ever visited, and who quite openly played solitaire or read at a table to the right of the front door. Like many Southwesterners, Mrs. Glass was as direct about another woman's house as a child would be about another child's toys, and she glanced about her with undisguised keenness.

Two glimmers caught her eye at once, almost as imperatively as lighted lamps in the long shadowy room. One was a silver—muffin-warmer, might it be?—on a low bookcase. With its fluted halves closed it would look like a giant seashell on legs; at the moment they were open flat and filled with pansies. The other was a massive gilded eagle glowing coldly from the fireplace mantelpiece at the far end of the room. The cruel profile, the half-hunched wings, the spread talons looked menacing even in frozen metal.

Mrs. Glass, who kept flowers in vases where they belonged, was somewhat confused by the silver object; she felt on firmer ground with the eagle, whose likeness she had seen reproduced in miniature on mirror tops. "Now I'll just bet that's old Colonial," she said, sidling closer and gazing up.

Mrs. Corey replied that it was—very old, in fact. After a nonplussed moment or two she invited her visitor to sit down.

Mrs. Glass did. Her blotterlike gaze had by this time absorbed a number of other things in the room; and now, added to her conviction that it was dangerous as well as pitiable for anyone to lead a hermitlike existence, there was a feeling she did not quite like to recognize. Mrs. Glass was impressed.

In the course of the next ten minutes she gouged from her hostess the facts that she was a widow, had spent her youth in the east, and—this came out very restrainedly—yes, she thought Griffin Acres attractive. Different, of course, from open fields across the main road.

"You must come and see our house," said Mrs.

Glass, having led her dexterously into this trap. "I have coffee on at all hours, and I know you'll like my neighbor next door, Helen Spenlow. She's from the East too. I'll bet you have all kinds of mutual friends."

A curious look flitted across Mrs. Corey's face. With a practiced gesture that somehow startled Mrs. Glass she lit a cigarette, and when she had finished it she began tentative rising motions. "It was very kind of you to call, Mrs. Glass, and now I wonder if you'll excuse me? I work in the mornings, you know."

Mrs. Glass gaped.

"I'm writing my memoirs," said Mrs. Corey.

"Of course they get that way—how can they help it?" said Mrs. Glass to Helen Spenlow. "But apart from the memoirs business she's quite bright, really, and quite intelligent. It's just a matter of getting her out and *meeting* people. Leave it to me. . . ."

On the following day she knocked again on Mrs. Corey's door. When it was opened she said heartily, "Got a coat handy? I've come to take you for a drive."

"Drive?" repeated Mrs. Corey. She looked astounded, as though automobiles had crept upon the century without her knowing it. "Where?"

"Anywhere." Mrs. Glass made a large gesture. "It's a beautiful day, much too nice to waste indoors, and you must have some marketing to do—I know I have. Come on. Do you good."

"Oh, no," said Mrs. Corey, and now she looked

almost frightened. "Thank you, but no. I have my work, you see."

"It won't run away," said Mrs. Glass indulgently.

A faint color appeared on the high papery cheekbones. "To tell you the truth, Mrs. Glass, I very seldom go out. I do not enjoy going out. I am very good company for myself. Besides," added Mrs. Corey with the weakness of courtesy, "I'm not feeling very well."

Not feeling very well, reflected Mrs. Glass as she retraced her steps on the overgrown path, and all alone in a house with no telephone. (She had checked.) That *was* dangerous. Suppose the old lady had a bad fall, or a heart attack? She looked hardy enough, but those were the very ones who went like a snap of the fingers.

Mrs. Glass at once set about making her a bland pudding.

That was on Wednesday. On Thursday it rained— a soft blowy rain that looked occasionally like snow because of the petals it swept from the apple and cherry trees across the road. Mrs. Glass, gazing idly out of the front window in her snug living room, was horrified to see the small sturdy figure of Mrs. Corey at work on the neglected lawn with—was it a hoe?

How the old seemed to court death! It might be understandable in a way, but it certainly was not Christian, and Mrs. Glass hastened into a raincoat and scarf and crossed the glistening street. In contrast to the neat and sensible crushed-stone and cactus which made up most of the landscaping of Griffin Acres, Mrs. Corey's efforts consisted of a wild-looking iris bed and daffodils scattered as untidily as broken pearls.

"My dear Mrs. Corey!" panted Mrs. Glass. "You'll catch your death of cold out here in the rain, really you will!"

Mrs. Corey, poising the hoe, gave her a penetrating look from under her white hair, wet and wispy at the moment but still piled as haughtily as though she were on her way to the theater. "I like being outdoors in the rain, Mrs. Glass. I'm very strong."

And she did indeed cut at the damp earth between the iris with a force that threatened the hoe handle. "Then you must let me help you," said Mrs. Glass firmly. "Let's see, have you got a trowel, or one of those little hand cultivators?"

Mrs. Corey gazed in silence at her erratic iris bed, and Mrs. Glass noted with a pang of compassion that the small face looked suddenly pinched to the bone. "I believe you're right," said Mrs. Corey in an exhausted voice. "I will go in after all. Oh, no—please, it's perfectly all right. I have a fire in the living room and I'll change my shoes at once. . . ."

But on Friday, Mrs. Glass's protective eye noted, the old lady did not appear outside at all, not even after the mail truck made one of its squeaky infrequent pauses at her box. Moreover, the window where she had often been seen playing solitaire was curtained, as though for an invalid's repose.

By two o'clock Mrs. Glass could stand it no longer. Scarfed and coated against the buffeting wind, she crossed the street, walked up the path, and knocked on the front door.

To another ear the utter silence inside might have had the quality of an animal's freezing in its burrow. To Mrs. Glass it represented the kind of natural disaster for which neighbors had been created. She knocked twice more, and when she had put her mouth close to the crack and called "Mrs. Corey?" without getting any response, she began to circle the house anxiously.

One curtained window after another confronted her, and complete stillness answered all her taps and calls. This, thought Mrs. Glass with the beginnings of indignation, was what came of elderly people shutting themselves off alone. Where were they then, when illness struck them, or serious injury?

She had become so inured to the thwarting folds of the curtains that she only realized belatedly that here, at the back of the house, was a sliver where they did not quite meet, and she was looking at movement inside the room.

It was a very small sliver, giving on a radiance that could only be lamplight. By squeezing one eye shut and concentrating fiercely with the other, Mrs. Glass could see a hand, unmistakably Mrs. Corey's, holding a lighted cigarette. While she watched, the hand lifted and the exhaled smoke came fuming down; then the cigarette was extended to an ashtray that was out of sight.

Mrs. Glass tiptoed away, although the wind that had undoubtedly smothered all her tappings and callings would have done the same for her footsteps. She felt much like a missionary at the sight of a leaping cannibal—shocked but infinitely compassionate.

It was quite evident what had happened. Abandoned to utter solitude, confronted for who-knew-how-many years by empty echoing fields, the poor woman had begun to lose her hold on reality. The very lack of another human voice would take its toll. Consider her fright at the notion of being taken for a drive, and her pathetic, "I do not enjoy going out. I am very good company for myself."

Griffin Acres had certainly come along just in time.

From then on, Mrs. Glass devoted herself unflaggingly to enticing Mrs. Corey out of her shell. She could not enlist her husband, who was taciturn and unhelpful, and her new friends, the Spenlows, had left on a vacation. In spite of the fact that Griffin Acres rang with the shrieks of children, the only young mother Mrs. Glass could get hold of, a Mrs. Demarest, said in a bemused way when told of the sociological problem across the street, "You mean she lives absolutely alone? Not another soul? How marvelous."

On the day after her eerie seclusion, Mrs. Corey, looking reassuringly normal, walked out to her mailbox, and Mrs. Glass was instantly there with a cake. To polite demurs about doctors and diets Mrs. Glass said robustly, "There's nothing in this to harm a fly. It will do you good, really it will. Oh, don't bother about that old plate—I'll just pick it up some day when I'm by. No, honestly, I must run now."

On the day after that, Mrs. Glass was struck by a

thought which should have occurred to her before. Mrs. Corey was lonely for someone of her own generation—of course! Someone to reminisce with, someone in her own position. Another widow.

Mrs. Glass's Aunt Mildred was considerably older than Mrs. Corey—Aunt Mildred was in her eighties, in fact, but she was a Senior Citizen of whom anybody could be proud. She belonged to the Matey Eighties and the Oldsters' Club in which last she had won a hornpipe contest last Christmas, and she had never lost her zest for the world around her. She was interested in clothes, and how much things had cost, and were those your own teeth? She was really very droll, bless her heart. No one, Mrs. Glass felt, could remain in a shell around Aunt Mildred.

Accordingly, she drove up to the Heights and fetched her aunt down for the day. It was calm and sunny, with almost drinkably deep shadows under the fully leafed trees—a day to lure even Mrs. Corey out. And presently she came, or rather went; it was only Mrs. Glass's vigilance which detected the small figure emerging at the back of the house, carrying what seemed to be a folded lawn chair.

"Oh, Aunt Mildred," said Mrs. Glass brightly, turning from the window. "I have a neighbor I'd like you to meet."

It went, Mrs. Glass thought, wonderfully well. Mrs. Corey brought out two more lawn chairs and Tom Collinses, and they all sat under the big cottonwood tree and chatted. Or they did at first; gradually Aunt Mildred's drink sent her into a beatific nap out of which she started galvanically at intervals, crying sharply, "Who? What did you say?" and then subsided into sleep again.

Mrs. Corey observed her thoughtfully. "What a remarkable woman," she said, and Mrs. Glass seized on this eagerly. "Isn't she? She gets so much out of life, even now. She's a little sleepy today—the drive, you know—but I can see she's taken to you. I think you two are going to be great friends. Yes, I'm sure you two—"

"Who?" demanded Aunt Mildred in a ratchety voice. "I heard what you said. I'm just—"

Her chin dropped again. Mrs. Corey smiled a little and rose. "I mustn't forget your cake plate," she said quietly, and went into the house.

Mrs. Glass roused her aunt, because the shadows were now lengthening, and they both thanked their hostess when she emerged with the cake plate. Mrs. Corey looked quite wistful at seeing them depart, thought Mrs. Glass triumphantly; indeed, her eyes, looking newly arched above and hollowed below, were almost sad. So soporific had the afternoon been that Mrs. Glass thought she heard her say, "It's self-defense"; but when she turned interrogatively, Mrs. Corey was gazing at the redwood wicker that enclosed Griffin Acres. "A well-built fence," she said.

Mrs. Glass's aunt was much taken with Mrs. Corey. She was reminded, she said, of a girl at a debutante ball in Chicago—just those hazel eyes and that cut of cheek; but the girl she was thinking of had run off with a ne'er-do-well, although she was of a very prominent family, and nobody had ever heard of her again.

"I must have her up to meet the girls," she said, and armed with her aunt's invitation, Mrs. Glass proceeded to the house across the way.

Never slack your hand in the day of battle, Mrs. Glass thought, and surely a dent had been made in Mrs. Corey's armor of solitariness. Not for nothing had the old lady looked so pensive, not for nothing had she given Mrs. Glass that special recognizing glance.

The sky was piled with clouds, so dazzling and close that one of them seemed to be peeping right over Mrs. Corey's roof. "You must have ordered this cloud," Mrs. Glass would say whimsically, "because—come and see—it looks just like your hair."

She sounded her knuckles loudly on the door—and surely Mrs. Corey had squirrels, because something was making a little gravelly sound up there. She rapped again, proprietorily, and never knew what made her lift her gaze to the tiny overhang of roof above the door.

The metallic gleam above was not the brass lantern that usually hung through a hole cut in the weather-stained board; no, it was the great gilded iron eagle, its head revolving a little although the day was still. How very peculiar, thought Mrs. Glass as the downward rush began; that wasn't there yesterd—

A Judicious Half Inch

Haddon saw the thing beginning to take shape before his very eyes on a day in July which seemed cloudless in every respect. He could even put an exact time to it, because he had just picked up his watch from the glass-topped table, timing the end of his therapeutic swim in his aunt's pool. It was exactly 1:45 P.M. when Chrissie Menlo slipped through the row of young trees that bounded the property to the north.

She was wearing a pink-and-white bikini that made her look a tiny sixteen rather than the six she was. All of her, in fact—her pointed petal-like face, her straight swinging ash-blonde hair, the setting of her light-gray eyes—gave her the air of an adult looked at through the wrong end of binoculars. Haddon, who had a basic distrust of young children who were always clean and impeccably dressed and who nipped deftly around at cocktail parties proffering canapés and bowls of nuts, disliked her heartily.

"May I go in now, Mr. Haddon?" asked Chrissie, cocking her head prettily. "You've finished your swim."

"In fifteen minutes," said Haddon, implacable.

Chrissie cast a rebellious glance at the pool, pear-shaped, still quaking bluely from Haddon's exit.

"Why does it have to be two o'clock?"

They had been over this ground many times before, and Haddon shrugged. "You know the rules," he said.

They were not his aunt's rules, as implied, but his own, and he was proud of them; the rules' very arbitrariness—that Chrissie and her brother Harvey could swim between two and three o'clock every other day—gave them the stamp of authenticity. His Aunt Ellen, in Spain for the summer, could hardly be appealed to.

Strong measures of self-defense were required with the Menlo children. They had evidently been brought up in the belief that they brightened the lives of all around them, and were welcome on any and every occasion for hours at a time. They sparkled with the conviction of their own worth, had been well tutored in the material value of things, and were as formidably boring as adults.

Haddon, whose recent leg wound in Vietnam had healed stiffly and imperfectly, had grown thorny when it became apparent soon after his arrival here that the Menlo parents were prepared, indulgently, to let him be their babysitter and pool guard for the summer. "He's depressed about his leg," he imagined them saying to each other, "and the children will take his mind off it."

Chrissie usually wheedled, however vainly. Today she did not. Dropping sociably down in another lawn chair she said, "My granny's coming tonight, from New York. That's my mommy's mother, not my other grandmother. She doesn't like to be called Granny."

"I don't blame her," said Haddon with feeling.

Chrissie gave herself a little hug in what seemed an essence of feminine malice. "Daddy said why did that damned old crone have to come now?"

It was clearly a direct quote, and Haddon was mildly diverted in spite of himself. "He didn't say this to your mother, I take it."

"Oh, no, he said it to his very own self," said Chrissie, widening her eyes in astonished recollection, "and he hit his desk. He must have hurt his hand. I asked him why he hit his desk and he said he just suddenly got mad at it." She giggled, glancing archly at Haddon. "Isn't that silly, getting mad at a desk?"

It was the kind of question, demanding the kind of response, that raised Haddon's hackles. He was almost pleased at the arrival of nine-year-old Harvey—brown, somewhat fat, with a large hearty face which would someday beam at Chamber of Commerce dinners. It was the boy's habit to inquire ceremoniously about Haddon's leg once every day, and he did so now.

"Will it ever get well?" asked Chrissie, not to be outdone in solicitude, and Harvey said reprovingly, "It's better than *no* leg. Right?"

"It's two minutes after two," said Haddon with inflection, and closed his eyes. Monumental splashes an instant later told him the children had dived in.

Perhaps because of his very annoyance at having his blessings counted for him so unctuously, his leg set up a gnawing ache. He lay consciously still in a dappling of coolness and warmth; presently, in a strange way lulled by the familiar pain, he almost slept. Birds twittered high in the branches of the sheltering cottonwood, mercifully absorbing the children's shrieks as they jumped and tussled in the water. Harvey's voice, when it came, seemed channeled startlingly into Haddon's ear, but the boy was only hanging onto the deck at the deep end of the pool, kicking his feet idly and saying, "Did Chrissie tell you about our grandmother?"

"She's coming tonight. Yes."

"That's not our grandmother who has a place at Lake Tahoe, though."

"With stables," added Chrissie, who had bobbed up beside her brother.

Both of them stared at Haddon with a kind of triumphant challenge. In command of this pool he might be, but could he ever possibly match a place at Lake Tahoe, with stables? Haddon's leg went on hurting. He said kindly, "There is absolutely nothing wrong with having stables on your property if they're kept clean. Horses have to stay somewhere, you know." And before their stunned faces could recover, "If you must dive for stones, use bigger ones. Pebbles get into the filter."

Harvey was of a more forgiving nature than Chrissie. He said as he wrapped his corpulence in a towel at the end of the swim, "I guess we'll be seeing you at six o'clock, Mr. Haddon. Mom said you were coming over for cocktails."

Haddon had forgotten about this invitation, acceded to three days earlier because there had seemed no graceful way of getting out of it. "Oh, I doubt it. With your grandmother coming—"

"Mom said to remind you 'specially," said Harvey,

bestowing a keys-of-the-kingdom look, and Chrissie, still cool but wanting him to have a taste of the delights in store, said, "I'm going to wear my nurse's costume that I got for my birthday, because Granny's never seen it, and Harvey's going to show her his bow and arrows."

"The arrows have rubber caps on them, for now," said Harvey at an involuntary expression on Haddon's face. "Because they could be very dangerous. Well, so long, Mr. Haddon. Thanks for the swim."

They skipped off hand in hand, a practice Haddon knew he should regard as charming but which he looked on sourly instead. He plunged back into the pool and swam steadily for half an hour, alternating crawl, breaststroke, sidestroke, backstroke in obedience to his doctor's instructions. Stretched out to dry on the concrete deck, he watched the sunny marblings of the disturbed water and saw, detachedly, a different and unpleasant pattern: the "damned old crone" coming "now"; the angry fist striking the desk; the bow and arrows; even, ridiculous though it seemed, the diminutive nurse's uniform.

Most significant of all was the fact that Menlo, apparently believing himself to be alone, had spoken that casually vicious phrase aloud. To do that he must have been driven indeed.

Apart from their being the parents of such children, the Menlos were pleasant enough. Barbara Menlo was a tall slender thirty, with short dark hair, an extremely long neck, and willowy shoulders. Her husband, Richard, was a good ten years older, with a face that belonged on a public-relations man, which he was—faintly humorous, horn-rimmed-and-eyeglassed, confident.

"Granny" was a surprise.

Haddon didn't know what he had expected of this relative, clearly downgraded in the children's eyes, but he was somehow startled to find Mrs. Fielding thin, tanned, calm, and very smartly dressed. It was only simple mathematics that placed her in her early fifties.

Damned old crone? Far from it, in any accepted sense, so that was the terminology of violent personal dislike, or bitter resentment. Or, coupled with the word *now*, fear.

Cocktails were on the patio. "We have to take advantage of this weather while we can," explained Barbara Menlo to her mother, "because it really blows in August and every tumbleweed in New Mexico winds up right here. And it clouds over regularly at four o'clock, although"—she turned, smiling—"I suppose I shouldn't be telling you all this, Mr. Haddon."

"Lessen the shock," said Haddon mildly. He glanced at Mrs. Fielding. "Do you live in Manhattan—the home of the brave?"

"Yonkers. Very different," said Mrs. Fielding. "Very small-towny, in a nice sense, if you've lived there as long as I have. Although now I—"

"Don't shoot the bartender, he's doing his best," said Menlo cheerily, gathering glasses out of startled hands. "Where's Florence Nightingale with something edible, may I ask? *Chrissie!*" he roared, and out she came, backing carefully through the sliding glass

doors from the living room with a silver bowl of nuts
and a plate of crackers and dip. She wore a navy cape
over a child-sized white uniform, and a frilled cap
which gave her the look of a ministering angel. She
said reproachfully, "It's *medicine*, Daddy."

"Sorry about that, Nurse," said Menlo jovially.
"Where's Harv?"

"Out putting up his target, of course," said Chrissie,
indicating with her chin, and indeed a small figure
could be seen in the distance, toiling back from the
ditch bank at the end of the Menlo property. "Would
you like some of these, Granny?"

"That's 'Grandmama,'" said Barbara in a steely
voice. "'Would you like some of these, Grandmama'?"

Chrissie inclined her prettily capped head and said,
"I'm sorry, Grandmama. Would you?" and Mrs. Fielding inspected the offerings with none of the flustered
overgratitude sometimes drawn forth from otherwise
sensible adults on such occasions. "I will have a nut,"
she said pleasantly. "Thank you, Chrissie." Obscurely, Haddon felt like cheering.

"We're all going to a horse show tomorrow," said
Chrissie, coming around to Haddon. "All Palominos,
they're the prettiest horses, and they only have it once
a year. Would you like to come?"

"Actually we're not, sweetie," said Barbara, looking
faintly worried. "Daddy and Grandmama have some
kind of mysterious appointment in the morning, so
they'll be using the car. But there's an Appaloosa show
next week, and I'm sure we can get to—"

"I hate Appaloosas," interrupted Chrissie in a clear
steady voice, "and Daddy promised. Daddy . . . ?"

Always neat, she set down her burdens with care and departed into the house.

Barbara said without much apology, "She's such a single-minded child. As a matter of fact, the horse show doesn't begin until eleven, so I suppose there's a chance—"

But Haddon's attention was on Mrs. Fielding, who had unobtrusively taken a pill from a small silver box in her purse and was gathering herself as if to rise. He said, "May I get you some water?" and she gave him a smile and nodded.

Haddon had been in the house before, and wended his way through the glass doors and angled to his right. Even if he hadn't known where the kitchen was, the tap of cracked ice and the sound of running water would have told him. From this perspective only a short stretch of counter was visible, with the drinks tray and Menlo's hands measuring and pouring Scotch over the ice in four glasses. There was also the entranced voice of Chrissie, obviously picking up an earlier thread: ". . . just a teensy-weensy bit sick?"

Menlo, finished with his bartending duties, raised a hand with the thumb and forefinger a judicious half inch apart. "Oh, about that much."

Out of sight, Chrissie giggled, a smothered spillover of excitement that affected Haddon like a fingernail drawn across a blackboard. There was something in the kitchen, he would have sworn it, that didn't belong among squares of late sunlight on the brick-patterned vinyl floor, the bowl of fruit, the blue pottery jar full of nasturtiums.

Menlo gave him an unruffled smile when Haddon

explained his errand, but Chrissie's hand had gone swiftly to her mouth. She jumped up at once and offered to bring the glass of water to her grandmother, but just then Haddon would not have trusted her with crumbs for a sparrow. He wondered, as he followed his host outside, what kind of pills Mrs. Fielding took, and why.

Twenty minutes later she told him. The Menlos seemed to take it for granted their guests were chafing to see Harvey's prowess with bow and arrow, and struck out energetically into the field at the sound of a distant hail. Haddon and Mrs. Fielding followed more slowly, and even before she said, "I think this is far enough for me," he had guessed that her calm was really a careful and necessary pacing.

"Heart," she said in a crisp dismissive tone, as though to apologize for public pill-swallowing. "Nothing very alarming, so long as I'm careful. As a matter of fact, though, I'm much more excited than I'm supposed to be, right now . . . You look like a good secret-keeper, Mr. Haddon."

Haddon assured her he was—and moved reflexively as Harvey, twenty-five feet away and apparently checking up on the attention of his audience, turned squarely around with his bow at full stretch. Sunlight shot along the length of the arrow, including the metal tip.

Menlo bellowed, "Damn it, Harv, watch that thing!" and after a second Harvey pivoted obediently and then released the arrow. Even from a distance its impact on the target was formidable, and Mrs. Fielding gave a little shudder.

"I hope they don't intend to let him aim that at birds . . . As I was saying, Mr. Haddon, Barbara doesn't know it yet because I want to surprise her, but I think I'm going to be coming out here to live. She's my only child, you know, and we've always been close. My doctor was afraid of this altitude for me, but he's found a medication that he thinks will lick that. I've been keeping my fingers crossed for a year, while Richard's been making some investments for me and looking around for a small house."

"And that's your appointment for tomorrow," said Haddon, smiling at her; her pleasure was contagious.

"Yes, he thinks he's found what I want. I really don't know what you make of me, confiding all my plans like this, but I had to tell someone."

"I won't say a word," promised Haddon, but as soon as he had spoken he felt a chill flash over him. With the mention of investments, Menlo's furious *now* might well be explained: how often before had men appropriated money entrusted to them, assuring themselves that there would be plenty of time to replace it? Or was Haddon merely prejudiced, largely because he didn't like the children? And even if he was right in his impression of a sharpening pattern, how could he, a near-stranger to this likable woman, warn her in a way which would not seem mad or monstrous or both?

Harvey had sent off his other arrows and was packing up his target while the Menlos and little navy-and-white Chrissie, anchoring her frilly cap with one hand, started back toward them. "I hope Chrissie won't let that uniform go to her head," said Haddon,

choosing his words with care. "I have a little niece"—
this was a firm and fluent lie—"who thought she could
really dispense medicine, and made the whole family
ill for a week."

Mrs. Fielding gazed at him thoughtfully. "Oh, I'm
sure Chrissie wouldn't do anything like that," she
said.

Haddon was pressed to stay for dinner, but he went
home. For the rest of the evening he told himself
variously that he had a suspicious mind; that it was
impossible to guarantee the safety of another person,
especially someone you had barely met; that Barbara
Menlo must know, in a general way, of investments
made for her mother by her husband over the course
of a year. He also convinced himself that, the change
in altitude notwithstanding, Mrs. Fielding's heart
condition could hardly be such that her sudden death
would pass unquestioned.

The ambulance left the Menlo driveway at 9:30 the
next morning, but the police cars were there for another hour. It was not until five o'clock that afternoon
that Haddon learned the exact sequence of events.

Chrissie (getting the last bit of mileage out of her
nurse's costume, reflected Haddon grimly) had dis-
pensed chocolate-covered mints after dinner, and they
had all retired early in deference to Mrs. Fielding's
fatigue. In the morning Barbara Menlo had tiptoed
out of the bedroom to wake her mother, deciding to
give her husband another twenty minutes of sleep

while she started breakfast, and then gone back to rouse him, and could not.

It was several hours too late for that.

And Chrissie had come skipping along the carpeted hall outside the door which her mother had instinctively closed, her gray eyes full of mischief. "I think we're going to be able to go to the horse show after all," she said, "because"—she held her lifted thumb and forefinger a judicious half inch apart—"Daddy's going to be just a teensy-weensy bit sick."

The Marked Man

OUTSIDE, in the cold rush of the night air, the left side of Walter's face felt iridescent with pain. The just-inflicted scratches seemed to seethe and simmer like neon tubing and at an occasional pair of oncoming headlights, he'd swing his head sharply out of the glare, as if he were summoning a laggardly dog in the shadows. His heart hammered as though he'd been running, which was the one thing he should not do.

The service station where the girl attendant lay unconscious on the floor—the girl who had astonishingly revealed herself as such only when her billed cap flew off with the suddenness of her jump at him— was now six or seven blocks behind him, and there was still no sound of a siren, no racing, revolving ambulance light. But the expectation of them was like an aimed gun, because although Walter had already disposed of the cheap dark mail-order wig, he was literally a marked man. For the first time in his life he needed a safe place to hide for a few days, and to find that he had to locate a telephone booth, and fast.

Gulping for air even at his only brisk walking pace, he arrived at a telephone booth at the entrance to a closed and spectrally lit shopping plaza. He ruffled through the L's in the chained directory, was seized

156

with panic when he appeared not to have a single coin, finally dredged up a quarter, dropped it in, and dialed. A kind of desperate confidence had carried him this far, but the moment of panic had undermined it and let in a thought that he had kept at bay since he'd fled from the service station: *What if Dex was out of town? Or had moved?*

His face flamed while he waited; he hoped viciously that the girl on the concrete floor was dead. Then an elderly female voice quavered a hello into his ear and he asked for Dex.

The voice hesitated. "He's—busy right now. Could I have him call you back—say, tomorrow?"

A party? No, but something was going on—he heard a low mutter of background sounds. "I'm just passing through. Tell him it's Walt," said Walter firmly, and a moment later the familiar voice was saying warily, unwelcomingly, "Hi, Walt."

A measure of Walter's usual cockiness came back, even in the middle of this crisis. Good old Dex, met at the reformatory in the southern part of the state, where Walter had been sent for aggravated assault and Dex for theft during one of his many flights from a broken home. Dex was twenty-four now, the older by a year, but like most essentially gentle people he was vulnerable. He was also married, with a baby, and assistant manager of his father-in-law's small but thriving grocery store. It had been very clear to Walter, who took care to keep in touch with anyone potentially useful, that neither Dex's prim little wife nor his hatchet-faced father-in-law knew of his reformatory past.

Now, tersely and without details, Walter told the other man that he was in a jam and needed a place to stay—garage, woodshed, anywhere—for a couple of days. Dex replied with the caution of someone with a listener beside him that he wished he could put Walter up but the fact was that his wife's mother had passed away the day before and Walter could see that, uh . . .

"Say, that's an idea. Your wife has lived in this town all her life. She'd probably know of some empty house for sale or something, wouldn't she, if you asked her? I mean if you told her it was for an old friend?"

For a dangerous interval of silence Walter was afraid he had gone too far with the implied threat. Then Dex said in a driven voice, "There's one place that might—where are you now?"

While he waited for the car, Walter tidied up the telephone booth, a process he had automatically begun while talking to Dex. Brought up by an elderly aunt as clean and joyless as bleach, further stampeded by the harsh institutional years, he had an active unease—almost a fear—of dirt and disorder. Although he himself was hardly aware of it, public places like washrooms and park benches and telephone booths were always the cleaner for Walter's passing. By the time Dex's car arrived, two cigarette butts, three matches, two gum wrappers, and a paper cup had been amalgamated into a small neat ball and thrown outside into a litter basket.

After a single instantly averted glance at the bloody marks on Walter's face, Dex confined himself to essen-

tials. The house he had in mind would be empty for
a week because the owners had gone deer hunting;
he knew this because the woman, a Mrs. Patterson,
had been in the store yesterday buying supplies and
he had heard her talking to the checkout girl. He
didn't think there was a dog. He had brought a flashlight. Beyond that, Walter was on his own.

As he finished these stony announcements a siren
commenced to shriek miles away to the south, the
urgent sound carrying on the cold dry air. Dex kept
his eyes unflickeringly on the road ahead, his only
and instinctive reaction a sudden pressure on the gas
pedal. Rejection came from him almost as visibly as
the simmers of heat from above a radiator, but he
said nothing until he pulled in without warning under
cottonwoods.

"Far as I go," he said then. "Second house on the
right. For God's sake watch it."

"Don't worry," Walter told him, confident because
of the distance between him and the siren. "You've
got nothing to do with this, right? Somebody else
overheard the woman and the checkout girl. So long,
Dex."

"Goodbye," said Dex tightly, and drove away.

It was a very good house for the purpose, twenty-
five yards back from the road, with at least that much
separation from its neighbors on both sides, and
cupped in trees. If the neighbors had dogs they were
the sleepy overfed kind: the only sound Walter could
hear as he advanced cautiously on the grass was a
faint twiggy rustle of wind high above him.

He melted to the rear of the house, his now-adjusted vision able to pick out details other than the black shine of panes. The back door was sturdily resistant; the windows appeared to be the kind that louvered out. Walter traveled along the wall and presently found another door opening on what felt like flagstones. The lock here gave with only a minimum of attention from his knife and he was inside in total darkness and utter silence.

A faint trace of perfume on the air, a fluffiness underfoot: although both were alien to Walter, he knew that this must be a bedroom. After moments of testing with all his senses—not that he believed Dex daring enough for treachery—he aimed the flashlight cautiously between shielding fingers, snapped it instantly off again, stood frozen with the image of the rumpled double bed still seared on his vision. The illusion of a suspicious householder risen to investigate the rooms within was fleetingly so strong that Walter's hand shot behind him for the doorknob.

But nothing happened; the darkness and silence remained tranquil. After a guarded moment he tiptoed through the open doorway that the brief spurt of light had showed him, found himself in a hall, and listened again. Then, because alarm had made his face blaze as though the girl's nails had just bitten into it, he fumbled his way to a bathroom, ran the cold water boldly, and held his dripping palms to it.

He had committed several robberies before this one, and in fact served a short jail term; but until tonight he had never used more than the threat of violence. He had never had to: his victims had the impression—

false, as it happened—that he was completely irresponsible, and heedless as to the consequences of his actions.

As a result, he was suddenly so exhausted that he did not even count the bills wadded deep in his jacket pocket under his gloves. He lay down on the unmade bed, faintly shocking to his neat nature even through his fatigue, and was asleep almost at once.

In the morning Walter took an appraising look around the bedroom and discovered that the untidy Pattersons were well-off—not that it mattered to him, as his object was to leave this place without a trace as soon as his scratches were healed enough to be disguised with makeup. He also learned that the money the girl had defended so wildly and stupidly amounted to $81.

. . . the girl who (the bedroom clock-radio informed him through the open doorway while he shaved and washed his damaged cheek with care) is still unconscious and in critical condition in a local hospital. Her head injuries indicate that she was flung with considerable violence against the corner of a metal filing cabinet. The robbery, which occurred at some time between 10:30 and 10:50 P.M., appears thus far to have gone unwitnessed. Police are continuing their inquiries in the area—

Walter turned the radio off. The fact that Dex had undoubtedly been listening to the news did not worry him in the least; if anything, the fact of the girl's condition would make the other man all the more sweatingly anxious that his own part in this never came out.

And when—and if—the girl recovered consciousness she could only describe her assailant as having
dark hair and brows. Walter's hair was fair, and without the burnt-match coloring his eyebrows were almost invisible. When the scratches had healed he
would be able to saunter down to the bus station,
retrieve his shabby suitcase from the locker there,
use his already-bought ticket to Denver, and be on
his way—free as air. Cheered, Walter set out for the
first time to explore his temporary domain.

Three minutes later he almost called Dex at the
grocery store; only the realization that it might be
dangerous for anyone to find this number busy
stopped him. Because something very strange had
happened in this house.

If it had been another kind of house, Walter would
have said jeeringly to himself that they had had some
party the night before. But in that case you would
expect to see liquor bottles about—and something told
him that people who lived in houses like this did not
give parties like that.

There were two bedrooms, apparently occupied by
children, besides the one by which he had entered,
and another smaller bath; a long deep kitchen, a dining room with three railed steps down into a big living
room; and opening off that, a den.

Everywhere there were costly looking mirrors and
rugs and pictures—and everywhere, drawers were not
quite closed on their brimming contents and cabinets
hung slightly open. In one child's room a sharp scuffle
had evidently taken place, knocking the sliding closet

doors off their runners and dragging the bedclothes half onto the floor.

Stunned, frightened, careful to stay out of range of the windows that faced the road, Walter checked the front-door lock and then the one in the rear. Both were firmly set. Then how—?

An echo of his own soothing words to Dex came back: "Somebody else overheard the woman and the checkout girl." Somebody had, and had got in somehow, and the thing right now was to make sure that they didn't return. His back prickling whenever he had to turn it on an open doorway, Walter explored deeper and found, in a utility room off the kitchen, a wall ladder which led up into a little room apparently used by a child at some time. There was a canvas cot, a vase of long-dead flowers, a faded cloth doll. And a door, now stirring gently in the morning air, that gave on the long flat roof and the accommodating branches of a cottonwood tree.

Kids, thought Walter with a great rush of relief as he fastened the hook-and-eye that secured the door. Seeing the Patterson family depart in a laden car or camper, deciding that the coast was clear for some casual mischief or vandalism: you read about such things in the newspapers almost daily. That explained the strange disorder below, and also the apparent lack of theft—Walter had counted two television sets, at least three radios, and a typewriter in the bedroom.

The active threat that the house had seemed to contain was now gone. Descending to the kitchen, Walter investigated the refrigerator and found the remnants

that a woman might decide were too little to take
on a camping trip and too much to throw away: half
a loaf of bread, a half stick of butter, four eggs, a
partly used jar of strawberry jam. No milk. Walter
drank his instant coffee black, scrambled two eggs,
and put jam on a slice of bread.

He cleaned up carefully after himself, not touching
the litter he found on the long cream-colored formica
counters; the earlier intruders, possibly known to the
Pattersons, might admit to the soup—there was a pot
with withering dregs—and the generous strewings
of orange peel. Distasteful though it was, Walter had
to leave the disorder alone.

And he would certainly not allow his nerves to
be ruffled by the untidiness everywhere else.

But it was a long day. The graveled crescent driveway crunched noisily three times—twice with cars
turning around, once with a panel truck disgorging
a boy who trundled around to the rear of the house
with a sack of whatever they put in water-softeners.
Walter held himself flinchingly still against a wall,
expecting a knock at the back door; but there was a
distant thump and bang and the boy returned to the
truck and drove away.

According to the three o'clock news the girl in the
service station, Emma Bothwell, had not regained
consciousness and was in surgery. A hospital spokes-
man said there was evidence she had marked her
assailant.

Angry at that all over again, Walter went and inspected his scratches, three and a trailing fourth. They
had dried and darkened a little, which he took to be

a healthy sign, and there was no spreading redness. He then roamed the house at a safe distance from the windows, and grimly did not restore to its rack a man's tie flung over one of the sapphire-upholstered dining-room chairs, did not snatch the weird collection of rubber bands out of the silver tray on the table, or brush off what looked like a wanton sprinkle of sugar on the table top.

At a quarter of five, because he would not be able to move about freely after dark, he opened a can of chili and ate it cold. At five o'clock the telephone rang for the first time.

The sound was terrifying in this refuge, carrying as it did a suggestion that someone was testing the emptiness of this house—or that Dex was warning him of imminent capture. But Dex would know that Walter couldn't lift the receiver. Dex would come himself.

If he had time to.

What if the Pattersons had cut their hunting trip short for some reason and had just stopped at Dex's grocery store for things like milk and butter and eggs? What if this were Dex with a helpless message?— "They're on their way home."

Walter had actually taken a step toward the telephone when it cut itself off in mid-scream. Some friend of the Pattersons who didn't know they were away, he told himself—telephones must be ringing constantly in empty houses—but he put on his jacket and stood tensely in the now-dark dining room, gazing through the half-drawn curtains at occasional passing headlights.

At the end of a long half hour he considered himself safe from this particular threat, but the deep uneasiness stayed with him and carried over into his sleep.

It was a cold windy night, and the trees around the house creaked with a sound like keys being inserted into locks. The faraway howl of a dog became a woman's advancing voice and brought Walter sitting up with his heart pounding. At some black hour later he came fully awake again with a thought that must have been hovering around the edges of his mind all day.

There was, he was almost sure, something called immunity—some means by which police protected informers. Walter's sole guarantee of Dex's continuing silence was the other man's fear at being an accessory; but mightn't the police shut their eyes to that in return for Walter, in view of all the fuss being kicked up about the girl? Dex wasn't very bright—anyone with brains would have told his wife about the reformatory at the outset, so as to remove that hold; but it might still occur to him that he could lead the police to Walter at almost no risk to himself. He might even emerge looking like a hero, reformatory or not.

By mid-morning of his second day in it, Walter had developed a personal hatred for the Patterson house. He had told himself that he would not let the general dishevelment get on his nerves, but in his restless wandering he yanked the door of the child's room shut; that was one place he didn't have to look at. A genuine rage at the marauders rose up in him, accompanied by a woolly feeling that he was missing some very important point.

Twice before noon he was startled by crunching tires in the drive, but although the cars passed close to the front windows they went by at undiminished speed. This seemed to be a natural turning-around spot, and Walter added it to his list of grievances against the house.

After his lunch—at least the pantry was well-stocked—he made the ritual inspection of his scratches and experimented with some liquid makeup he found on a bathroom shelf. The scratches stared through, and the trouble was that they did not look like an encounter with a cat or some barbed wire; they looked exactly like what they were. Walter added another layer of makeup and thought that by tomorrow night . . .

The one o'clock news, which he watched on the television set in the curtained bedroom, jarred him to total attention, because the girl in the hospital was holding a news conference. With a thin prominent-jawed face surmounted by bandages, she looked more like a boy than ever. Blurred backs kept getting in the way as she spoke—eerily, for this was the first time Walter had heard her voice.

"I think he was about twenty-one or twenty-two. He had dark hair. He had on a dark jacket—I don't remember what color his pants were. Yes, he was wearing gloves, darkish gloves I think," she said to some off-camera question, "and when he told me to give him the money he took one glove off, I don't know why. I jumped at him, because I knew my uncle kept a gun in the desk—that was behind him—and I thought—"

Walter had stopped listening. He was staring at the television screen in a paralysis of horror. Once again, in a sick dream that sent the blood to his face and made the scratches flame, he felt the tiny menacing prick in the palm of his right glove as he opened the office door—was it a tumbleweed thorn? In the same awful slow motion he watched the girl's submissiveness at the cash register, although he hadn't known she was a girl then, and saw himself remove the glove with its threatening little stab so that he could more securely take the bills she was about to hand him.

But no matter how hard he tried, he did not see himself put on the glove after that lightning attack. Instead, he felt the dry slither of the money he had fumbled out with his bare and shaking hand.

What had he done then? Closed the cash drawer? Touched anything else? Out of that tiny interval of unexpected violence and pain and everything gone wrong, it was impossible for him to remember.

As though he could silence the girl forever, Walter leaped to the television set and snapped it off. His hands had begun to tremble, and he locked them tightly together and walked calmingly up and down. *This* was the blurry issue he hadn't quite grasped earlier, this was what had to be faced. Would the Pattersons, returning to their untidy house, accept it for the mischief it was—or, having picked up a newspaper or listened to a car radio, assume at once that a fugitive had been in hiding here, and send for the police?

Walter's fingerprints were a matter of record, and there was hardly a place in the house where he hadn't left them. The robbery would be secondary to the police by now; they would be haring after him for aggravated assault, at the least.

Wait. All this presumed that the Pattersons found their home in this shocking condition. What if they *didn't* find it in a shocking condition? Walter certainly couldn't leave it exactly as they left it, but first impressions would probably be clouded by the commotion of a return with children. By the time Mrs. Patterson's eye fell on something odd in the arrangement of her ashtrays or frying pans, Walter's fingerprints would have been smeared and overlaid and polished out of existence.

With a vast relief he began to clean up the house.

It was a staggering job, but his spirits began to lift as he got the surface disorder—the straggling tie, a ball of string, the bunched rubber bands, an empty flowerpot—out of the living and dining rooms and into what he hoped were appropriate places. With a little forcing he coaxed drawers and cabinets to close everywhere. When he had swept the floors, the rugs seemed to have a visible overlay of tiny confetti-like debris and he had to get out the vacuum cleaner.

The cleared tops of tables showed strange little sticky places which required sponging, and only the extreme urgency of his situation made Walter tackle the worse of the two children's rooms. His ingrained vision here was of taut tight mitred sheets and blankets, with toys and games, if any, tucked out of sight.

It did not include spilled popcorn, an empty Coca-Cola can stuck jauntily in an open bureau drawer, or a yawning closet which looked as though it had been stirred by an eggbeater.

It was almost dark when Walter finished, but the dining-room table gleamed, the living-room couches were unsullied, the floor shone. The house would certainly not have passed the antiseptic eye of Walter's aunt or the grim glare of the matrons in the reformatory, but nobody entering it would cry out in shock. Exhausted but pleased, his nerves quieted by the new orderliness, Walter consumed a can of the Pattersons' soup and went to bed.

In the morning he heard, but was not alarmed by, one more turning-around car that crunched, paused, and crunched away again.

Anne Merrick had swung her little car briskly into her sister's driveway. The hunting trip, irresistible to the Pattersons, would be followed in less than a week by a visit from the senior Pattersons, a gentle and elderly couple from New Jersey who had never been allowed to see the house in its normal state. There were things to be done before even the stoutest-hearted cleaning woman could be brought in. Anne had volunteered.

The Pattersons lived in a manner uniquely their own, only partly explained by the fact that Betsy was a free-lance writer. They had tree surgeons to minister to their trees and sent their Orientals off to be cleaned at the proper intervals; occasionally, after some unheralded visitor had happened in on a scene of chaos, they laid down stern rules for their three young children: no eating in the living room, keep your bedroom tidy, hang up your clothes.

For perhaps forty-eight hours both the children and the parents observed these strictures, and then fell back into their cheerful disorderly habits. Once every six months, for a week at a time, Betsy Patterson and a cleaning woman attacked the bulging closets and brimming drawers, and then the tranquil process of deterioration began all over again.

Anne, remembering the condition of the house three mornings ago when she had helped Betsy and Rob and the children get packed and away, thought now that a fast hour ought to do it. She wasn't aiming at actual cleanliness, after all, but only at the impression that rational people lived here. Bare surfaces were marvelously deceptive. If she made a lightning sweep through the living room and the dining room, with the curtains at its low window half drawn to reveal the shining black walnut table and the immaculate sapphire chairs. Anne's hand stopped sharply before taking out the ignition key.

Three days ago the dining-room table had worn a heavy sprinkle of salt—Adam, the youngest of the children, could never pass a salt-cellar without upending it—but now the table gleamed. So did the silver tray, innocent of the rubber bands dumped into it at the last minute because Betsy had said firmly she would not travel in a vehicle containing children *and* rubber bands. And what had become of Rob's discarded tie, which Anne remembered clearly because the burgundy and gray stripes had looked so decorative against the sapphire chairs?

For a sickening second it was almost as though the Pattersons themselves had been wiped and polished away. Anne's impulse was to race out of the driveway; instead, because it seemed imperative for some reason, she forced herself to leave at the same speed at which she had entered. Two minutes later, at a telephone in the next house, she explained matters to a bewildered voice at the Sheriff's office.

"*Not* ransacked, you say," repeated the deputy uncomprehendingly; without knowing it, he was much in Walter's position. "Then what seems to be the trouble?"

"The trouble is that my sister's house *always* looks ransacked, and now it *doesn't* and there has to be something very wrong," said Anne, unfairly impatient. "There's been someone in there, don't you see? I wish to heaven you'd hurry. They might still be there—"

Walter was feeling almost tranquil as he applied a second coat of liquid makeup to his nearly healed cheek; the order around him, after the antic condition of the house, was like balm. Even when he heard a brisk sound from the region of the front door, a sound of entry, his heart gave a horrible knock but he did not panic.

A friend or relative with a key? The Pattersons themselves, returning earlier than planned? No matter; his foresight and drudgery of the night before had insured against an immediate alarm, and he had a choice of two rear doors.

He used the door in the bedroom, closed it sound-lessly behind him, backed over flagstones into the chest of a man as careful and quiet as he. But this one—how could it *be*, after all his labor?—this one had a badge and a hand at his holstered hip.

Change of Climate

ONE LAM CHOP," wrote Chloe Carpenter in her diary on an evening in late June—at nine years of age she had, and would have all her life, a natural talent for misspelling—"one baked potatoe, some string beans, a pice of apple pie." She studied the last item and then, because caret marks were still in her future and this was to be a very exact account, she crossed it out and wrote, "a small pice of apple pie."

Hester Carpenter had no idea that her daughter was keeping this meticulous record of Hester's food intake—fortunately; it would have made her self-conscious to the point of being unable to eat at all. But Tom Carpenter knew about it, and was both touched and approving. It seemed to him the day-by-day log of a miracle, although that was the very word he was supposed to avoid.

"Oh, she'll do better in the Southwest, no doubt about it," the doctor had said two months ago in Massachusetts. "In fact, to put it baldly, I doubt very seriously if she'd survive another winter here. But I have to warn you, Tom—after the first dramatic improvement there still may be difficulties. Chances are she'll acquire new allergies, and then there's always the existing damage. You mustn't expect a miracle."

Hester had never been really strong—it was her

174

look of almost luminous fragility which had first caught Tom's eye; but she had not developed asthma until a year after their marriage. Or perhaps it had been there for some time, masquerading as frequent attacks of bronchitis and a faint but noticeable shortness of breath after activities like climbing stairs. In any case, the asthma had become sharply worse after Chloe's birth. At first there were seasons of the year when Hester was entirely free of it; gradually these periods shortened, and pneumonia began to make its appearance.

They saw a parade of specialists—bald and conservative, young and daring, whose advice, with minor differences, came to much the same thing in the end: avoid the known allergens—among them, cat dander; pursue a dust-free routine in the house; and "learn to live with your illness."

Surprisingly enough, until Chloe was seven years old, they managed the last instruction almost as easily as the first two. Hester was determined not to become a professional invalid, or to make a martyr of her husband and a slave of her small daughter; and for a long time she succeeded. She hoarded her strength in unobtrusive ways; on bad days, when the sound of her breathing was like a loud and steady filing, she retired to piled pillows behind her bedroom door.

She had grown up in the small town of Falcon, Massachusetts, and Tom did not have to worry about her being lonely while he was at his office and Chloe at school. Girls she had known since high school dropped in, and neighbors made morning visits for coffee, usually bringing along a sumptuous homemade pastry at which Hester could only nibble. Chloe, arriving home at three o'clock, leaped enthusiastically into her role of "house-woman"—"Housewife, do you suppose she means?" Hester asked Tom, laughing—and polished everything that could possibly be polished: vases, candlesticks, tabletops.

As a result, the little house glowed more than the prescribed dust-free routine demanded; it held a concert of personalities as undivided as a clover. Hale and hearty visitors went away with an illogical feeling of envy; they said, "There's nothing like trouble to bind a family together," but they knew it was more than that.

When Chloe was almost eight, Hester had her first bad attack of pneumonia. Six months later she had another and worse one, shrouded in an oxygen tent while Tom spent two tormented nights at her bedside and the nurses smiled at him with terrifying cheerfulness.

He made the decision then, knowing that it meant giving up the well-paid job which had enabled him to meet the medical bills; giving up their home and their friends. Although it was not really a decision at all in the sense of choosing between alternatives, because it was clear now that there was no alternative. While Hester convalesced, much more slowly than ever before, he quietly organized the move to the Southwest.

June turned and became July. Hester had gained six pounds, and her pearly skin was acquiring a faint tan. The one unfortunate side effect from the change of climate—sinus trouble, which the doctor assured them could be alleviated by drops—seemed a small price to pay.

Chloe had been her mother's anxious companion for too long to let go all at once, but little by little, as Hester grew stronger, Chloe explored a world strange to eastern eyes—a world with fleet little blue lizards, roadrunners, and even, in the landlord's back field, an aristocratic but friendly horse that came promptly up to the fence for the carrot or apple she brought. In spite of the wanderings which seemed to her boundless, but were actually contained in less than a half acre, Chloe was always in the driveway to greet Tom when he got home from work.

She was there on a late afternoon in mid-July, wiry, sunburnt, and clearly bursting with something. When Tom asked his ritual, "What did you do today?" she said excitedly, "Oh, Daddy, I helped Mrs. Whitman tear up all her flowers. Look!"

Tom did not merely look; he gaped, appalled. Mrs. Whitman was the other tenant of the duplex apartment, a pleasant gray-haired woman whose chief preoccupation seemed to be the deep brilliant border that edged her little lawn on three sides. The border was now bare drying earth, the flowers themselves a heap of ruffled and shriveling color piled up outside the gate.

To Tom, for just a flash, the child looking up at him seemed to have the wanton triumph of a small boy standing with his slingshot near a shattered greenhouse—and then Chloe was saying defensively, "The flowers, I don't know which ones, made Mother sneeze and her eyes puff up, so Mrs. Whitman *said to*."

Hester was tranquilly regretful. "It's too bad about Mrs. Whitman's garden, isn't it? I felt awful, telling her about the doctor's orders—you know, to sit out in the sun for a little while every day—but she understood perfectly; in fact, she couldn't have been nicer. I came right in and baked her a batch of brownies."

Tom, remembering the weeks of Mrs. Whitman's assiduous weeding, cultivating, watering, sent a look of wonderment at his wife's back. Did Hester possibly think that a confection hastily whipped up in the kitchen—? No, of course she didn't; she had simply made a small token apology in the only way she could on the spur of the moment.

. . . But, he thought later that night while Hester slept, her breath quiet and even, she had been mistaken in thinking that Mrs. Whitman had "understood perfectly." That brutal heap of uprooted flowers, piled there openly by someone who loved them, was a statement of cold anger only emphasized by the invitation to the complainant's child to come and help with the carnage.

It was too bad in every sense, because Tom had hoped that Hester, so used to the daily companionship of other women, would start making friends in the neighborhood. His last waking reflection, still troubled, was that it might not be a bad idea to have Chloe, an avid car washer, surprise Mrs. Whitman tomorrow or the next day by scrubbing her little cherry-red Volkswagen . . .

When Tom hinted worriedly to Hester about her possible loneliness, she denied it cheerfully. Her friends back East had been marvelous, and of course she missed them; but it was a positive luxury now to be able to do, unassisted, so many of the domestic things they had helped her with before. And of course—here she glanced around vaguely—she had Chloe for company.

But this, although it was not borne in on Tom immediately, was less and less the case . . .

The doctor was enormously pleased with Hester's progress, and she apparently took this as *carte blanche* because, by the time August had arrived, she was seldom still. Wearing Bermuda shorts, a thing she could not have done before because of the sticklike thinness of her legs, Hester took down and washed and rehung the venetian blinds; she carried out the scatter rugs to air. She also washed the windows, inside and out, scoured the oven, and began on the paintwork. If the apartment did not have the warm glow of the little house back East, it was at least very shiny.

Tom did not find it surprising, in view of Hester's steady gain, that Chloe had stopped keeping her diary; the last entry, for July 26th, was: "Steak, asparagis, mashed potatoes, vinila ice cream." He now had a small but annoying problem of his own: his sinuses had evidently become affected by the dry heat and at night, frequently, his forehead felt bound with iron.

Hester's wonder-working nose drops, trickling bitterly down the back of his throat no matter how carefully he administered them, did not seem to help.

One night in mid-August, when he was cautiously
congratulating himself on feeling fine, the tense pain
came creeping back at the dinner table. Maybe a storm
approaching, thought Tom; the sky looked thunder-
ous and he had sensed electricity in the air ever since
his return home from work. Well, they needed the
rain—

"Eat your dinner!" said Hester in a voice that made
Tom's fork jump in his hand. He glanced at her as-
toundedly—she had delivered the words like a cuff;
but her attention was on Chloe, fair head bent, hands
in her lap although they were having roast chicken,
which she loved.

"Eat your dinner," repeated Hester more quietly
and perhaps more dangerously. The storm which
Tom had thought so innocently to be in the upper
elements was closer, and he was so bewildered that
he could only stare.

"I'm not hungry," said Chloe, the corners of her
mouth beginning to waver helplessly, "I feel sick."

"Very well, then, you're excused," said Hester ev-
enly, and held herself remorselessly still and attentive
while the child pushed back her chair, dropped her
napkin, bumped her head on the table in the course
of retrieving it, and then fled.

The door of her bedroom closed. Hester sprinkled
salt and said calmly to Tom, "You look tired—was
it a rough day?"

"Not bad," said Tom distractedly, putting down

his own napkin and starting to rise. This was like a dream, in which elk went by in Easter bonnets and nobody thought it odd at all. "I'll go see what's the matter with—"

"Chloe is sulking because that foolish horse is gone," said Hester casually, and proceeded to tell him.

Tom had been aware of the affection between Chloe and the horse in the next field, and knew that the landlord let her mount occasionally and go for blissful ambles. As the horse was trained to halt the instant the weight in the saddle began to slip, it had seemed the most innocent of diversions. What Tom hadn't known—"I hate being such a constant nuisance to everybody"—was that Hester reacted badly to close contact with horses, and had begun to wheeze when Chloe came in from her rides.

She had, she said, forbidden Chloe to ride the horse, but at every opportunity the child had slipped over to the fence to caress the white-blazed face and brush the dark-gold mane dedicatedly. "—which came to pretty much the same thing," said Hester ruefully. "Mr. Lacey saw the problem right away, and said his son would be delighted to keep the horse at his place—it doesn't get enough exercise here anyway. Somehow, I expected Chloe to understand."

Or understand *perfectly*, like Mrs. Whitman with her flowers? Tom was shocked at this disloyal thought—they were here after all for Hester's health, and allergies were not to be played around with; but his forehead now felt sealed with pain. When he had eaten what he could of his dinner he picked up Chloe's untouched plate. "I think I'll bring this in to her now."

Hester's eyebrows rose, but all she said was, "If you think it's wise."

Chloe got over the horse, as Hester had sensibly predicted she would, and settled herself to the serious business of making friends in the neighborhood before the opening of school. This was not the automatic process of a child who had been constantly with other children, but an almost adult approach. As a result, she was home at noontime for a sandwich and milk, usually with a standoffish and staring little girl in tow.

Tom took his headaches to a doctor, was informed that his sinuses were as clear as a bell, and, although he kept it from Hester so that she would not worry, he began to take the tranquilizers the doctor prescribed.

Hester bloomed, even in the scorching heat. Her delicate tan had turned brown, and she was strong and rangy. She was busy making new curtains, busy registering Chloe for school, busy waxing the floors, relining the kitchen shelves, taking down and washing the ceiling light fixtures. She had grown used to, as Tom and Chloe had, her own newly nasal voice, although she would say irritably now and then, "I sound exactly like a duck."

Although it was only the end of August, the annual weather prophets were out in force. Tom and Hester, who could seldom find any news of Massachusetts in the local papers, nevertheless learned with guilty pleasure that an early and very hard winter was predicted for the East.

(But how warm and snug the little house in Massachusetts had been, with Hester on the couch in a pretty housecoat, Chloe bustling importantly in the kitchen, Tom peacefully reading the evening paper while the wind raged outside and the fire simmered and snapped on the hearth. Lamplight over everything, and a perfect security that had nothing to do with locks or bolts or storm windows.)

We are all happy, Tom informed himself, swallowing his white pill; the pity is that we didn't do this sooner.

School was to begin on August 29th. On the 27th, coming home with the commissioned notebooks and pencils and lunch box, Tom saw that Chloe had washed Mrs. Whitman's car again; the little red Volkswagen was dripping and flashing in the sun. And there was, mystifyingly, a cat fight in progress somewhere close by. Of all the things Hester couldn't have near her . . . How could a cat have gotten—?

He was alarmedly out of his car and inside the gate when the menacing shrills became distinguishable words instead of rising and falling howls. "—*so* nice of you to be sweet and considerate with the neighbors," shrieked the cat voice. "Never mind me, *I* don't count. But how many times have I told you about those filthy sneakers? And look at those shorts. You've been in the wading pool with those dreadful children, haven't you, Miss? I said, *Haven't you, Miss?*"

There was an odd sound then, not a response from Chloe but still a sound. Tom's stupefied eye caught a lunge past the screen door; his ear heard a panting, "There you stay!" and then a sharp bang.

The bang seemed to split the frontal bones of his head. Standing paralyzed on the path, at once incredulous and certain, he realized that this strident plunging creature in Bermuda shorts was his gentle luminous Hester, this contemptible "Miss" his skinny worshipful child.

He made himself go in. Hester was washing lettuce at the sink, her hands unsteady. There was no sign of Chloe. Tom said with a weariness he did not know he had accumulated, "What's the matter?" and Hester whirled.

"You'll have to talk to that child, Tom." *That child.* "She's always been spoiled, but now she's completely out of hand."

Spoiled. The nine-year-old who by now was an expert at doing dishes, ironing her own clothes, compiling bizarrely spelled shopping lists, and trudging faithfully around supermarkets . . . "What's she done?"

"Disobeyed me, deliberately. There are some very dubious-looking children up the street who have a wading pool, and I told Chloe that she was not to go there."

"Hester, this was a hot afternoon—"

"That's not the point. The point is that I told her not to," said Hester, spacing the last five words almost softly. By contrast, pots and their lids leaped into a clattering frenzy under her hands when she turned to the stove, and the glance she flung at Tom was razorish with—was it anger? Or some perverse excitement? Something, at any rate, that changed her into the kind of woman you saw dragging a small sobbing child ruthlessly by the hand, jerking all the harder when the child stumbled.

"I think we'd better get it clear here and now that I won't stand for this kind of behavior," the stranger at the stove was saying in her nasal and driving voice. "If you don't punish her, I will."

There were still a few shafts of late sunlight in Chloe's prim little room. She lay on her bed with her back to the door, not so much crying as shuddering, taking convulsive breaths which she buried fiercely in the pillow. Tom sat down on the bed and turned her gently to face him; he had to glance away quickly for a moment, feeling his own throat prickle at the dull red mark on her cheek.

That was the curious sound he had heard. From outside.

He had meant to tell Chloe quietly and reasonably that she could not disobey her mother, making it—because he realized suddenly that in the past week or so they had understood each other very well indeed—more of a father-to-daughter warning than a parental thunderbolt. But the reasonable words would not come; so he simply sat there, stroking the tumbled hair away from her forehead and talking about small detached things until she was able to heave a very deep breath with only the barest tremor.

She said, "Mother doesn't like being better, does she."

It was neither a question nor an accusation. It was an observation delivered with adult despair, and it encompassed much more than a hard humiliating slap.

It took in the last—three weeks, four? Tom could not be sure, in his shock at the nakedness of the words, any more than a man could be sure when, after living with an obscure pain that frightened him, he was asked by the doctor who put an exact finger on the source, "How long have you had this?"

He didn't—at the moment he couldn't—answer his child. He gave her forehead a final pat and walked to the window, where he gazed out blindly into the coming dusk.

Was it possible? Could Hester have acquired the last allergy of all, and be no more able to assimilate health than cat dander? Were there personalities who could not thrive, or thrive sanely, on physical well-being?

It was appalling to think so, but it was less spine-touching than the notion that this personality had dwelt inside Hester all along, and had simply never been well enough to come out before. How, in that case, it must have raged and struggled against the tranquillity and binding love in the little Massachusetts house . . .

Tom's shoulder muscles gave a quick cold ripple as he shook that off and went back to the first possibility. If their past happiness even in the face of illness had been so present in his mind, how much more so must it have been in Hester's? Certainly she had never consciously liked being a semi-invalid, but—the stream of solicitous friends dropping in, the cheerful little gifts of a crocheted bed jacket or a homemade coffee cake, the momentous gaining or losing of half a pound—and, yes, the attention.

Chloe had been her devoted shadow, but now, like any other healthy nine-year-old, Chloe roamed and played. And Hester had flung herself into frenetic activity, perhaps battling unconsciously with this terrible new allergy before it began to win.

Tom had never asked, but he was coldly sure now that Chloe had admired and helped in Mrs. Whitman's garden. She had worshiped the friendly horse. She had set about making friends, to prepare herself for entering a strange school, and been invited to wade in a backyard pool. The sacrifices to Hester had not been voluntary, or even appeasing, but they had certainly been made.

And yet . . . Hester will be as upset as I am, said Tom to himself.

Hester was not. Told falsely that Chloe was asleep, she said with an edge, "Funny how easily she falls asleep on nights when we have meat loaf," and attacked her own dinner with zest. It was very good meat loaf, and a few small bites of it settled in Tom's stomach like the best cement; Chloe's vacant place at the table, and the silence from her room, pressed upward against his ribs.

Although Hester said nothing further about punishing Chloe, her face was curiously set, and when she asked Tom after the dishes were done, "Aren't you going to take your usual walk?" he manufactured a yawn and said, "Too tired."

He was, of course, not worried about any small

personal action which might be taken in his absence down the long driveway. Certainly not. He was simply—tired.

He lay awake all night—not like someone with merely restless intervals, but literally all night. Once he got up quietly to look in at and cover Chloe; for the rest, he listened to his wife's deep untroubled breathing and studied a number of scenes which unwound like tape against the black ceiling.

In the morning he said cheerfully to Chloe, "Come on, I'll buy you a new dress for school," and to Hester, "They're having some kind of executive session at the office and I don't have to be in until eleven."

Surely Hester did not look somehow impotent as they left?

"Daddy," said Chloe hesitantly in the car—she was pleating the fabric of her skirt incessantly, a new and disturbing habit—"won't Mother be mad because she didn't come too?"

"She's got a million things to do," Tom said airily, and bore her off to the back-to-school department of a downtown store. He found a reliable-looking saleswoman to whom he gave vague suggestions about a dress, and told Chloe firmly to wait for him there.

There were public phone booths on the first floor, and from one of these Tom sent himself an urgent telegram signed with the name of his former employer in Massachusetts; he would be home to open it when it arrived, so that no question would be raised as to its place of origin. To make doubly sure, he instructed the operator to have the message delivered; there would be no one at that telephone all day, he said.

From the phone booth, because it was somehow of immense importance that Chloe should not even uncomprehendingly hear what he was going to say, he proceeded to the railroad station. Judging by a few banners strung about it was "Sunshine Appreciation Week," which was just chasing out "Eat More Cottage Cheese Week." When he asked the pretty clerk at a ticket window for two and a half fares to Falcon, Massachusetts, she said with arch reproachfulness, "Oh, surely that's round trip, sir?"

The buoyancy assumed for Chloe's sake had left him. Perhaps as a result of his sleepless night his ears resounded queerly with the doctor's voice: "To put it baldly, I doubt very seriously . . ." and the prediction of the weather prophets.

There was nothing momentous in the glance he sent through the ticket window. To the pretty clerk, who remembered him for approximately a minute afterward, he was just an ordinary, pleasant-looking man; fair, thirty-fivish, rather tired, with lines around his mouth. There was certainly no special inflection in his voice when he said, as though arousing himself from a dream, "No—that will be one way."

Point of No Return

It was so astonishingly fast and simple that for a few moments Roger Corbin could scarcely believe it. He had brought about the most tremendous of all changes—the transition from life to death—and it had been almost like slapping shut a book in a fit of boredom. But then Vera's thin faded-blonde hair had obviously covered a thin skull.

The goldfish in their tank saw everything, and after a quick molten scurry they resumed their tranquil flickering through painted china arches and clusters of imitation white coral. They, and much later an unseen kitten at the edge of a dark field, were the only witnesses to the final disposal of Vera Corbin, and neither would ever speak . . .

In the morning, the face in the bathroom mirror certainly did not look like that of a wife-killer's. The really sinister husbands—or so Roger Corbin had come to believe through novels and television—were the meek and rabbity kind, or the smooth and too-handsome, or the saintly pillars of the community.

He fitted into none of these categories. At a vigorous fifty-three, his big hard body and tanned square-jawed face under the close-cut gray hair were testimonials to his liking for the outdoors. Women, looking at the jaw, sometimes suspected a temper there, but they suspected it in the mysteriously intrigued and admiring way in which women often notice failings in any husband other than their own. Men were dryly amused at Roger's caution with his money—his luncheon companions usually left a surreptitious additional tip—but they liked his easy outspoken air and respected his shrewdness.

Less was known about Roger's wife, who spent a good deal of her time making complicated casseroles and polishing her ivy, but on the surface at least the Corbins had a reasonably normal twenty-five-year marriage. It was true that Vera, like many small excitable women, had been known to rush off in a huff for a week or so at a time, but this was regarded as a kind of substitute for bowling or ping-pong.

As a result, no one at the office was surprised when Roger let it drop in a half-annoyed, half-humorous way that he wished his wife would get over her current fit of pique and come home again. Howard Cooper and Dennis Thorne, married colleagues who prudently wanted no details of a domestic upset, merely raised their eyebrows and shook their heads noncommittally. It was left to doting Miss Wegby, Roger's secretary, to register her sympathy and indignation by a number of moist warm glances and, the very next morning, by a yellow rosebud from her mother's garden.

Miss Wegby might have been designed by a committee of jealous wives. Although only in her late twenties she had the overbosomed, broad-hipped figure of a matron twice her age. She was asthmatic and nearsighted, and in vain she administered layers of powder to her gleaming and earnest face, a practice which someone had unkindly likened to hiding her light under a bushel. But she was an expert shorthand typist, devoted and passionately loyal—she frequently took work home with her—and she was more comforting to Roger Corbin at this juncture of his life than any houri. Because hadn't someone said that no one knew a man as well as his secretary? And here was Miss Wegby bringing him boutonnieres, and Danish pastry for his mid-morning coffee—"You can't be eating properly, Mr. Corbin"—and generally cherishing him to the top of her bent.

She need not have worried about Roger's meals. He did think a little wistfully about Vera's casseroles—for a woman of almost no imagination she had been an extremely good cook—but the freezer was well-stocked and his appetite had never faltered. He would return to the silent house at 5:30, set his dinner preparations in train, feed the knowledgeable goldfish with a steady hand, and settle down comfortably with a drink and the newspaper. Half-hearted dinner invitations had been conveyed through their husbands by Mrs. Cooper and Mrs. Thorne, but Roger had declined. "I'd better be at home, just in case . . ."

Far from getting on his nerves, the empty house delighted him: it had somewhat the quality of a finally stilled faucet. Not that he took any liberties with the housekeeping: he was fully as property-minded as Vera had been, and used coasters and place mats and ashtrays with care. The cleaning woman had made her weekly visit, and a half hour every evening with dustcloth and mop kept the place almost as gleaming as when Vera had been in residence.

When eight days had gone by, he invited young Derek Bingham, the only unmarried man in the office, for dinner; he had done this before in temporary bachelorhood and it was important to keep to the pattern. More than that, it was time to plant the first suggestion. Over an after-dinner beer, gazing pensively at the hearth where Vera had fallen after her head was sent crashing back against the stone edge of the mantel, he mused like a man thinking aloud. "Maybe we ought to get away more, weekends. Vera and I," he explained to Bingham's somewhat baffled face; they had been talking about Vietnam a moment before. "Maybe that's what's been the trouble."

Bingham looked uncomfortable, and studied his beer as attentively as though it had just spoken to him.

"Oh, no real trouble—good lord, you don't throw twenty-five years out the window," said Roger with too much cheerfulness and too much confidence. He brooded. "I guess the damn columnists are right and a woman gets feeling taken for granted. I thought she was all wrapped up in the house"—his gaze swept over the textured lemon carpeting, the gleams of mahogany, the pictures selected to match the slipcovers—"but . . . well." He slapped the arms of his chair decisively and made a wry face. "Those are deep waters, and you haven't even got your feet wet yet. Don't let it put you off that very pretty girl I saw you with at lunch today. How about another beer?"

Predictably, Bingham fled.

The first move had been made.

If Roger should presently announce tidings of a divorce, who would gainsay him? Not family; Vera's widowed mother had died ten years before and Vera had quarreled bitterly with some cousins who had sheltered the old lady and been remembered in the modest will. They had received the money and Vera had inherited two paltry lots in a slum section of Newark, New Jersey, and since then there had never been so much as an exchange of Christmas cards.

Close friends were not a hazard, because Vera had had none. After their eleven months here Roger was far better known than she, and if he did not raise a hue and cry, who would? It was not as though he intended to remarry; Vera had cured him of that. Neither were there any financial considerations. They had a joint checking account, but at some future and judicious time he would simply change banks. Although he and Vera had made out mutual wills at the time of their marriage, unrevoked through the years of corrosive dislike, he wasn't losing anything there. To any questions he would merely say—and it must often happen this way—that his wife had severed all communication with him and he had no idea where she was to be found.

. . . Found.

Unlikely, in the newly plowed field ready for planting two miles away. Roger did not even know the owner, which seemed in itself a safeguard. As for

Vera's old green Volkswagen, driven deep into the trees along a ditch-bank and containing the suitcase she had packed so furiously with her own hands—the car was far more likely to be stripped, in that area, than reported to the police.

And if it were reported? One more case of a woman foolish enough to have picked up a hitchhiker, or to have driven at night with the passenger door unlocked. Volkswagen and body were well over a mile apart, but surely the police would waste considerable time in dragging the obvious place, the ditch. They could investigate the house and Roger to their hearts' content. There had been surprisingly little blood on the hearth where Vera had stood and said the one unforgivable thing, and he was confident that his own small-hours' scrubbing, the cleaning woman's ministrations, and several open fires had taken care of that. As to his own life, the deepest probing could not produce any indication of monetary gain or any interest in another woman, because neither existed.

And there were certainly no witnesses to the growingly acid domestic scenes, the peculiar deadlock about divorce although there had been no religious barrier. In Vera's world divorced women were subtly disgraced—and in a community-property state Roger was grimly determined not to part with half the reward of his thirty years' work. They were bound forever by their wall-to-wall carpeting and copper-colored kitchen appliances and Vera's philosophy of life, of which perhaps the high point was an insistence on cloth napkins instead of paper.

Why, the police would have to ask themselves,

would a husband of twenty-five years suddenly not
be able to stand it a single moment longer?

Roger had once read somewhere that by tracing a
finger gently and unceasingly over the same place
on the skin it was possible to produce bleeding. Vera
had done that, only at the end she had not used a
gentle finger but the sharpest kind of knife . . .

Roger Corbin was an only child, his father dead
before he was born. Marguerite Corbin was an attractive and ambitious woman who found her adoring
son an asset until he was twenty-five and a distinct
liability thereafter. Was this great and prematurely
graying creature to contradict her punishing diets,
her facials, her cunning hair tints? She found Vera
Beasly, and said to Roger in her fluttery voice, "Darling, it isn't *right* of me to monopolize your life—
it's the kind of thing that gives mothers a bad name.
I would like to see you settled down, you know, perhaps in the kind of home where"—she smiled at him
bravely—"I might some day be welcome now and
then."

A little bewildered, frightened at his mother's mysterious air of courage, Roger had married Vera, small
and energetic and blonde. Mrs. Corbin, unencum-
bered, presently went off with a dubiously titled Ital-
ian and sank, along with all hands, on his yacht off
the coast of Sicily.

Vera was all twitters and comfort, and alluded only
three or four times to the fact that, far from leaving
an estate, Mrs. Corbin had bequeathed them a few
debts. She took a course in shorthand and typing,

got a job in a wholesale drug house, and at the end of five years was office manager. The rise to this position was reflected at home in a new and critical crispness, a sharper eye on time-wasting habits like a late Saturday-morning sleep. Roger, beginning to make a respectable income, was also beginning to feel like an erring typist. He insisted that Vera give up her job.

A mistake? Possibly, because her new aggressiveness was now unleashed at home. On the other hand, she had been well on the way to becoming a small female dictator, with "absenteeism" and "waste motion" routine parts of her conversation. Deprived of a public outlet for her energy, she sat back triumphantly to see just how well Roger was going to provide for them, and the fact that he did so with increasing success seemed to gall her.

At the end of ten years there were no children, a fact at which Roger was by now obscurely relieved. Vera was less reticent, but for a different reason. "There's so much in heredity, and, well, we know about my people but we don't know a thing about your father, do we? I mean, perhaps it's just as well . . ."

This carried a deep sting which Roger was careful not to let his wife see. As a child he had asked the usual questions about his father, only to be confronted by a pretty little handkerchief applied to his mother's eyes. "My treasure mustn't ask me about that. Such a wonderful man, such a tragedy—oh, I simply can't talk about it!" Once she indicated that his father had pined away of tuberculosis; on another and forgetful occasion Mrs. Corbin mentioned a fire in a theater where he had given his life to save women and children. Long before her death Roger had accepted the strong possibility that he was illegitimate.

Far from undermining his devotion to his mother's memory, the delicate insinuations about any irregularity in her marital status only deepened Roger's dislike of Vera, already well begun. If it had become hatred at that point, or even if Vera, perversely, had not been such an excellent manager, the marriage might have come to a quiet and bloodless end. But his aversion was still like a familiar but scratchy sweater—nothing to make a man rip the garment off— and in Vera's careful hands their net worth was becoming very comfortable.

So the point of no return was reached, unnoticed, and passed. The negative aspects of their marriage were in a curious way as binding as their possessions. Vera could not complain that Roger drank to excess or abused her physically or gambled or ran around with other women; indeed, he did not even run around with her, and this formed the basis for her furious little departures. To her querulous demands as to why they could not go away occasionally for a vacation—even a weekend at some nice resort—Roger merely answered implacably that he was going fishing or hunting instead; surely it had penetrated even her head that some kind of physical exercise was considered imperative for men of his age?

It was incredible to him that she should seriously expect him to spend time and effort and money to closet himself in a strange place with a woman who was only and barely tolerable in seeing to his comforts at home. And because it was so very obvious he never bothered to say it.

For his part Roger could not point to any neglect of the house, or any frittering away of money. Nor had Vera let herself go. At forty-nine she was nothing more than plump and well-girdled, and she dressed with fussy care—so much so that no collar or pocket or waistline ever suited her, but had to be smoothed and plucked and tugged at with office-manager firmness. Apart from two small deep vertical lines between her eyebrows, her skin was still almost girlish; her blonde hair, although faded, was carefully curled. It was a tribute to the Corbins' peculiar expertise and perhaps to their surroundings that, on the rare occasions when they entertained, Vera's wifely little sharpnesses and Roger's sardonic retorts made them seem all the more solidly and comfortably married.

On that evening eight days before, up until the very last seconds, they would not have had the appearance of killer and victim . . .

It had not been a good day at Slade Enterprises where Roger worked. At 4:30 he even had occasion to snap at the usually faultless Miss Wegby. Arriving at the foot of his driveway at 5:30, in the moodiness that springs from remorse, he discovered that Vera had failed to bring in the newspaper and that it had been run over by some vehicle with disastrous results. He had backed and swerved with grim speed and driven to the nearest store; returning at 6:00 with an edition from which the owners of the store had

torn the pages containing their own and their com-
petitors' ads, he was informed by Vera that dinner
would be ready in a matter of minutes.

Roger's blood pressure had slid up a notch. For
the last several weeks, in her disapproval at the fact
that his pre-dinner Scotches were gradually creeping
from two to three, Vera had been stealthily advancing
the dinner hour. "Well, *I* won't be ready in-a-matter-
of-minutes," he had said shortly, mimicking her brisk-
ness. "After having to go nearly back to town to get
the blasted paper I'm going to have a drink in peace."

Vera's brows went up at his use of the singular,
but she only said, "I'll do what I can with the chicken
hash"—in a tone implying that she would put down
some kind of insurrection—and departed for the
kitchen.

She was back almost at once, her arms folded militantly. When Roger did not glance up from his muti-
lated newspaper she said in a high bright voice, "I'm
sorry about the paper, it must have been the dishwasher repairman. It broke down this morning and
I called them at once, and of *course* he didn't come
until mid-afternoon and of *course* he didn't have the
proper part on the truck and of *course* it was too late
by then for him to go back to the shop and get it.
All this charming *mañana!*" finished Vera with biting
scorn. "Why, I wonder, is it considered so charming
to be lazy and late about everything but the bill?"

All, so far, had gone largely according to pattern
except that they were both a little more tense than
usual. The finger-snapping, efficiency-watching Vera
simply did not fit into this leisurely suburb, reflected

Roger, forgetting his own temper at delay, and periodically she went off into these diatribes. "If this is a prelude to suggesting that we move back East, forget it," he said, walking to the kitchen to make his second drink. "We've got a lot of money invested in this place. My God, look what you've got here!"

His gaze swept appreciatively over hanging ivy and copper and stainless steel. "I have looked. A broken dishwasher," said Vera, prim and icy.

The quarrel, although it was hardly more than routine procedure, continued through dinner and after. Both said what they had said a hundred times before, and Vera's face acquired a mottled flush; she was not a woman, if such a woman existed, whom anger became. They had reached the familiar point of, "If you're so bent on going away, why don't you? Nobody's stopping you," and "All right, that's exactly what I will do!" when Vera added something new. Flinging a sponge dramatically into the spotless sink, wheeling to pass him, she said with quiet deadliness, "Do you know something, Roger? I'm sure nobody at the office would dare tell you, but you are getting *very odd.*"

On that she had departed for the bedroom. Thump, click, rustle: she was packing like a wet hen, until the ultimate respectability of a husband should appeal to her again. Roger interjected a fresh note of his own, shouting through the closed door, "Do me a favor and take a lot of clothes with you. Along with your bank book."

In one sense this savings account was a thorn in his flesh as it was solely in Vera's name and not subject to the community-property law, representing income from the New Jersey lots left to her by her mother. On the other hand, it financed these little expeditions of hers.

Ostentatiously, while the sounds of preparation went on in the bedroom, he finished his coffee, consulted the paper, switched on the television set. He was the picture of unconcerned comfort when there was a suitcase-sounding thump in the entrance hall and Vera, gray-suited, wearing a small black-and-white hat and black pumps, stalked past him across the lemon carpeting to the mantelpiece.

"I'm leaving Mrs. Tafoya's key here. If you want her to clean on Thursday, put it under the middle pot of ivy outside the front door."

"What . . . ? Oh, the middle pot. Right," said Roger, gazing sedulously at the television screen. Vera, one white glove on, was now smoothing on the other with the tiny interminable pushings that accompanied this act. Her anger was almost as visible in the room as a shimmer of heat. "Shall I tell you something else, Roger?"

"Do. I have always lacked the Beasly culture, and stand ready to be instructed. I have never," said Roger—Vera's father had owned a small feed-and-grain store—"quite understood the difference between chick feed and mash."

He was on his feet—polite, receptive. Vera's face hardened and she lifted her head. "I've finally figured out why your mother never told you about your father. She obviously didn't know who he was—don't you *dare* touch me, Roger Corbin, don't you dare lay a fing—"

That was when the goldfish began their molten scurry . . .

Barring any immediate family or close friends to make an outcry, people were, Roger discovered, rather easily lost. Now that he paid attention to the subject, the newspapers seemed full of tiny casual items about bones stumbled across by hunters or picnickers or exploring children.

Vera's mail, for instance, presented no problem. Advertisements from local stores, a card advising Vera that her dentist had moved his office to a new address, a darkly worded statement that two library books were overdue. Roger found and returned the books and paid the fine to a high-school girl he had never seen before.

The way now seemed clear, particularly as young Bingham could testify to his presentiments, for a rueful announcement that he had heard from Vera in Reno and she meant it after all: she was divorcing him. "Twenty-five years," he would repeat, shaking his head unbelievingly, but he knew from experience that his acquaintances would shy away from details and his secretary think him the most wronged of men.

It was the sheerest accident that he did not carry out this plan. Returning uncustomarily to the house at noon one day because he had forgotten his reading glasses and automatically scooping the mail from the box, he took a cursory look before he left. Mortgage payment, electric light bill, a political circular—and a letter, airmailed, for Mrs. Vera B. Corbin from Paget & Maybank, the Newark attorneys who handled the rental property.

A thorough scrutiny with the letter held against the light told Roger nothing except that there was no check enclosed. But in this climate envelopes came unstuck with ease, and with only a little coaxing this one did. In his speculation over the lack of people who might make pressing inquiries about Vera he had forgotten all about this area of her life, and the omission frightened him; his fingers were trembling as he unfolded the single stiff white sheet.

And learned that the two insignificant lots had stood in the way of a new bank building and parking lot under an urban renewal plan. Thanks to Vera's already-sent power of attorney, the sale had been consummated for $50,000.

Roger did not dare take the afternoon off—it was something he had never done before—but he looked at production records and signed the morning's dictation in a daze of rage and bewilderment. $50,000! How could such a thing possibly—? But of course it was Vera who visited the mailbox on weekdays and she had simply sequestered everything that had to do with the sale of the lots. Business-minded, she knew very well that this windfall did not come under the community-property law, and she had kept the earlier bargaining stages secret.

What else—*who* else—might there be that he did not know about or hadn't thought of?

Back in the house at 5:30, the house that might be

teeming with destructive forces, Roger did not even pause to make a drink but commenced a search at once. He spent very little time at the desk where Vera had paid the household bills and written letters and Christmas cards; she would have kept nothing clandestine there. The bedroom? That was the obvious place—or no, it wasn't. The kitchen.

The letters from Paget & Maybank, four of them in a period of more than a year, were curled neatly in the innermost of a nest of cannisters in the cupboard under the sinks. Besides being lodged behind an almost impenetrable barrier of frying pans and chafing dishes, the cannisters were vessels Roger would never use no matter how long he cooked for himself.

On the heels of panic came a kind of appalled fury at Vera. It was safe now to pause for a drink, but clearly she could not be trusted one inch. By midnight, however, with three more drinks and a gulped-down hamburger along the way, he had searched the house so thoroughly that he was confident there were no more secrets.

Today's letter no longer frightened him in itself; it asked no questions and did not even require an acknowledgment. And four communications in over a year did not suggest that Paget & Maybank were feverishly preoccupied with the affairs of Vera B. Corbin. As they had her power of attorney, it might and probably would be months before they instituted any inquiry as to the whereabouts of their client. Months before Vera was found dead and her will became effective and $50,000 passed into Roger's bereaved hands.

He snatched his mind from that thought as he would have snatched his hand from a high-tension wire.

But it came back, and with it, like the frill on a lamb chop, came the idea of triumph over Vera. But first—and Roger shuddered when he recalled how close he had come to announcing that he had heard from her in Reno—first he must consider the risks.

Provided that Vera were disinterred quite soon, the date of her death could be established to have been substantially earlier than the glad tidings from Paget & Maybank, so there was no real problem of motive on his part. As to the actual disposal of her body—unflinchingly, he sent his mind back.

A small woman, she had fitted quite easily into the back seat of her Volkswagen. It hadn't been late—not much after 9:00—but he had been met by very few oncoming cars and, in that quiet area of alfalfa fields and tiny adobe houses, had been passed by only one. The headlights had died around a curve; he had sat tensely in the Volkswagen to make very sure of that before pulling in at the edge of the plowed field.

The mewing kitten? A dog would have worried him, with the vision of someone at the end of a leash, but people here did not walk cats. On the contrary, they abandoned unwanted ones.

It had taken a surprisingly long time to dig deep enough, even in the loose earth, and more time to fill in, moving backward on hands and knees and raking roughly with his fingers so that the earth should not look tamped down. In the dark he could only guess at his success. Then off to the ditch a mile away, the green Volkswagen driven deep into green, and this time there were no headlights at all and almost no house lights showing. It had been a long walk home, again without encounter.

The car. That was the safe and indirect way. Arrange to have the car reported, so that the police would come to him with the initial disadvantage of having to deliver gravely disturbing news. An abandoned car, a suitcase packed as only a woman could pack it, the ditch . . .

In the morning Roger cruised by the ditch, gazing with an informed eye through the mask of tamarisks and cottonwoods. The Volkswagen didn't seem to be there, oddly, although even by night he could not have been mistaken—

Dangling binoculars casually, he left his car, pushed his way through undergrowth, gazed disbelievingly at heavy tire tracks in the sandy soil. At the time he had thought complacently that the Volkswagen would be stripped of its tires and battery and possibly even its engine, and that there would be a juvenile conspiracy not to report the car to the authorities.

But they had taken, or towed, the car itself—the whole car. And with it Vera's suitcase, the tangible argument that she had left her home of her own volition. Car theft thrived in this locality; the Volkswagen, its engine number filed off, was probably spray-painted behind somebody's house.

But the suitcase: what had they done with that? Combed it for valuables, emptied it into the ditch? *That* was a sweat-producing thought; although there were no edible fish to be caught, little boys might well be out with rods, perhaps hooking a blouse or a slip, running proudly home: "Look, Mom!"

With the vanishing of the car Roger was a man reduced to a course he distrusted and feared, and on too-short notice—but the $50,000 beckoned, and there was now the threat of premature discovery as well. He would have to do what countless men before him had done: humble himself before the police, tell them that his wife had left him after a quarrel, and that he feared for her safety.

He would do it from his office. Calling about such a matter from such a place would have an open, above-board, nothing-to-hide air . . .

He was spared the trouble. His detour, plus a wild sand-ridden wind that made driving slow and parking lights necessary, brought him to Slade Enterprises late. When he entered his office, Miss Wegby, spectacularly sallow in maroon, was apparently bidding good-bye to a man in a deputy sheriff's uniform.

"Oh, Mr. Corbin, you're just in time," she cried asthmatically. "I know this gentleman is only doing his duty, but it's so ridiculous! I've just told him that Mrs. Corbin was in yesterday after closing hours to pick up the money for her trip."

The room took a small lurch before Roger Corbin's eyes. He made himself look directly at the deputy. "I'm afraid I don't understand. Has there been some question . . . ?"

"You know how it is," said the deputy ruefully; he studied his shoes with embarrassment. "New administration, new broom. We get a call from some

catty female to see is your wife all present and ac-
counted for, and we have to check it out. I tell you,
we get all kinds. Well—" He touched his wide-
brimmed hat. "I wish they were all as easy as this.
Morning, ma'am . . . Mr. Corbin."

Roger could not move at once; an abyss so deep
and black that he could not even begin to see the
bottom of it had just opened up in front of him.

Loyal Miss Wegby. Snapped at on the day that mattered, rushing over to his house in her car with the
missing report, seeing him depart with Vera's body.
Passing him on that dark quiet road, stopping at a
careful distance, coming back.

Watching.

She was eyeing him steadily now. Vast-bosomed,
broad-hipped, sallow, asthmatic, she was giving him
a look which contained far more than secretarial devotion—a look of yearning love. Because of the high
winds and her asthma, her breath made little mewing
sounds, like an unseen kitten at the edge of a dark
field . . .

The Pool Sharks

THEY CAME knocking at the door just as she was getting ready to leave for the hospital: two dark-eyed, dark-haired children she hadn't seen before in the month of living in the new house.

"Can we go swimming?" It was the boy, perhaps ten or eleven, holding his younger sister's hand with a firmness that suggested a frequent guardianship. Their fringed and upturned glances were hopeful but wary, in case of a rebuff, and Sarah smiled at them in spite of her own distraction.

"Well, not today, I'm afraid." She was careful not to explain that there wouldn't be anyone here for the next few hours, because the temperature was in the mid-nineties and with the confidence of childhood they wouldn't worry in the least about swimming unattended; it would strike them as much more fun. "Where do you live?"

The two round dark heads nodded obliquely across the field, which meant around the corner. What with the bulldozer and the cement mixer and then the various pickups with the company's name on the side, they had probably known to the minute when the swimming pool was completed and filled. (Tom had said, yesterday, "We'll probably have to establish some kind of rules, with the only private pool in the neighborhood, but let's face that when we come to it.")

Sarah suggested eleven o'clock the next morning, waited for a cautious few minutes after they were out of sight, then forgot them as soon as she was in the car.

It was only the second time she would be visiting her husband in the hospital. The first had been before dawn, when after what seemed like hours in the waiting room she had been allowed to go up to the fifth floor. She knew by that time that Tom's terrifying middle-of-the-night collapse had been caused by a bleeding ulcer, but she was still unprepared for his total pallor and the visible effort it cost him to open his eyes and smile faintly at her. It was clear that at this point her presence would do more harm than good, so she kissed him, drawing a black look from the nurse whose possession he now was, and said simply, "I'll be back."

In the corridor, following her out, the doctor was blunt. "It's a good thing you got him in here when you did, Mrs. Birchall. He's going to need another transfusion, and I want someone to have a look at his heart. Better wait until two or three o'clock this afternoon before you come in."

Meticulously, Sarah had split the difference; it was 2:30 when she left the elevator on the fifth floor of the hospital, followed the room-indicator arrow to 523, and felt an actual slam in her chest at the white-stubbled, scooped-out face that turned wearily on its pillow as she entered. But—of course—this was a semi-private room and Tom's bed was the far one;

she hadn't registered that fact in the small-hours panic.

She rounded the dividing curtain, and a lesser shock awaited her. Tom wasn't sitting up as she had somehow expected but was lying flat and vulnerable, and although the dark suspended bottle was gone he was still very pale and his hand, when she took it and held it hard as she bent to kiss him, was cold.

She said, fast, "Tom, you look so much better. I've brought"—she produced the small suitcase—"your robe and slippers and pajamas and things." Her eyes were beginning to fill, and she turned briefly away as though a nurse had started into the room. "And some stupid damn cherries and books. How do you feel?"

"Better. Really, better," said Tom, speaking in the light and careful way in which a man with a murderous headache might talk. "This is an awful nuisance for you, driving all the way in." He closed his eyes and opened them again. "Did you have a swim? Christen the pool?" This time his smile was less effortful. "Better hurry up."

Sarah was three and a half months pregnant, although she had tried on her bathing suit the day before and no one would have guessed it. "Not yet, I'm waiting for you. As a matter of fact, though—"

She realized belatedly, with a kind of buried shock, that she could not present Tom with even the tiniest concern right now; she could not say that neighborhood children had already asked to swim in the pool which did not yet have its protective fence; could not inquire if they were insured against the kind of accident that might happen even if she were on the scene.

Depleted though he was, Tom was gazing at her and waiting for her to finish the sentence.

"—I imagine the water is fairly nippy, coming straight from the well," said Sarah, "and I wouldn't mind giving it a few days under the sun first. When does the doctor think you can come home?"

Tom hadn't seen his own doctor yet, although three different ones had gone into a huddle over his electrocardiogram. He thought he would have some kind of word around seven o'clock, when the doctor apparently made his rounds. He said, "Don't drive all the way back in tonight, Sarah," and nodded at the telephone beside his bed. "I can call you."

"So you can," said Sarah, and they both understood that she would be back there that evening.

Louis and Marisol—the girl's name was new and delightful to Sarah—arrived promptly at five minutes of eleven the next morning. Sarah was ready for them, bathing-suited in case she had to jump in, giving them, briskly, a few elementary safety precautions. They were not to run on the deck, or push each other into the pool. Although the water was nine feet at the deep end, they were to be careful diving and each to make sure that the other was visibly well out of the way.

She supposed as she spoke that she had the kind of unheard drone of their own mother, or teacher, but without Tom she felt a sharp concern in this particular situation.

They could swim; she made sure of that before she left the pool's edge for a basket chair under the trees where she could watch them while pretending to read. Louis had a sturdy windmilling stroke, Marisol, who had all the breath of a mosquito in her tiny two-piece suit, was less splashy and quietly determined.

Sarah gazed at them in a detached way; she had something new to think about.

Tom had had a wildly uneven heart-beat on admittance to the emergency room, and although the electrocardiogram had shown no sign of damage, the doctors were not quite satisfied and were attaching a monitor. Even in the event of the favorable outcome they cautiously expected, it would be at least a week before he could be discharged from the hospital. In the meantime he mustn't be worried in any way, but of course Mrs. Birchall would appreciate that.

. . . After an hour, with a little shrill dissension toward the end of it, Louis and Marisol climbed out of the pool, toweled themselves dry, bundled their belongings expertly onto their bicycles, and departed. Sarah only realized after she had said "Goodbye" that they hadn't been going to say anything at all. Swim, wrap-up, finish—as though it were a municipal pool. Oh, well, they were only children and maybe—cover-all excuse—they were shy.

They weren't shy. Sarah was making herself a glass of iced coffee late the next morning, as the most palatable way to drink the milk the doctor had ordered, when Louis and Marisol rounded the corner of the house. This time they were accompanied by two older boys, fourteen or fifteen, who stared appraisingly

about them as they sauntered over the grass. One
of them caught Sarah's eye through the kitchen window, appraised her as well, and kept on going.

She felt a quick, surprisingly sharp flash of anger.
She had intended a pre-lunch swim—Tom had said
last night, "Promise me you will. It's the least you
can do for yourself with the heat and all your driving"—but that wasn't it. It was a feeling of being
used, and used with a certain amount of mockery
which said, "You're rich. You'd better fall over backwards about sharing your pool."

They weren't rich. They had only been able to buy
this place because it was in need of so much basic
repair, and more sensible people would have applied
Tom's inheritance from an uncle to a lifetime roof
for the house, a new heating system, and a remodeling
of the smaller bathroom. Tom and Sarah had thought
it all over and decided on a temporary roof job, sweat-
ers, and a little shivering for the first winter, guests
who wouldn't mind the bath as it was—and a swimming pool.

She put down her glass of iced coffee, her heart
beating quite hard and fast, and went outside. It was
hot, she reminded herself, and after all what was there
for these kids to do, miles outside the city in the tail-
end of the summer when simply not being at school
was no longer enough?

Louis and Marisol and one of the older boys were
already in the water. Sarah registered the fact that
the other boy was not wearing swimming trunks but
a pair of jeans which did not look particularly clean.
Sarah thought conscientiously: Maybe they can't af-

ford—and the boy removed a wrist watch which had cost far more than a bathing suit, threw her a casual grin, and jumped feet first into the pool.

Sarah walked down the deck to where Marisol, who was infinitesimally more responsive than Louis, was sitting on a step. Sarah said pleasantly, "Are these your brothers, Marisol?"

For some reason this was very funny. Laughter erupted from the pool, accompanied by sidelong dark glances, flashing teeth, flung-back wet hair. It crossed Sarah's mind that, hair or not, they looked a little like dangerous fish. *Stay friendly.* In five or six days Tom would be home, and he would know how to handle this. She managed to keep the careful balance in her voice. "Then introduce me, will you, please? My husband's coming home for a swim at noon and he'll want to know who our visitors are."

The two pointed faces stared up from the blue water as if they knew no English at all, or they did but considered their names to be none of Sarah's business. "He's Frank," volunteered Marisol, pointing, "and he's Jimmy."

Something decided Sarah not to press the matter further. These new arrivals were also able to swim, so she went back into the house and stayed within earshot. It wasn't difficult; Louis and Marisol were far more boisterous in the company of their older friends, and the pool rang with shouts and huge splashes and simulated screams. If they had been more likable boys Sarah would have gone out and said, "Would you try to be a little quieter, so I won't think someone's drowning?" As it was, she bore the assault on her nerves until one of her frequent glances out the bedroom window showed her what was now going on.

They were all milling around the deep end of the pool while the older boys—Sarah had a reluctance to use their names even in her own mind, as if that implied a tenuous friendship or at least acceptance—cannonballed into the water, scrambling up the ladder again with an assembly-line effect. With a vision of one of them landing on spindly little Marisol, she went rapidly outside and said firmly after two attempts to make herself heard, "Don't do that, please. It could be quite dangerous."

There was a peculiar pause, indicating that she might or might not be obeyed. Louis and Marisol clung to the edge and gazed expectantly up at their friends, one of whom had been poised for another knees-tucked leap. It was a matter of face. But that was saved by a shrug, a brief and indistinguishable mutter, an impish—smile? No, a grimace—and then the boy's exaggerated daintiness as he sat down on the deck and lowered himself into the water. Laughter all around.

And all wrong, thought Sarah dismally, retreating to the house again because to sit in the basket chair and watch them openly would be to pose a challenge which they might very well meet. She had grown up with sisters; she didn't know how to treat boys.

Boys, or premature men?

She kept her occasional vigil, folding laundry on the bed—would they never go home?—and presently saw the jeaned one scramble out of the pool, consult his watch, gaze curiously at the house, and jump back in again. She glanced at the bedside clock. It was 12:20, and she had said her husband was coming home at noon to swim, and they were going to wait until he did.

Instantly, furiously, she got into her suit and a terry robe, caught up her bathing cap, and went outside. She said with a steady smile, "Sorry, but it's time for my swim."

They all got out at once, and it was absurd to think that was mockery too, as though she had been an overseer appearing with a whip. The pool thermometer had been wrenched from its nylon tie around the ladder's hand-rail and lay on the bottom near the drain. It wasn't an earth-shaking matter, but the fact that they hadn't even bothered to dive for it was enough to make Sarah say casually, "By the way, no swimming tomorrow. We're superchlorinating the pool."

We, evidence of strength. And a mistake, as the first of a long line of excuses. ("We're expecting guests to swim all day. My husband has a terrible case of impetigo. We're keeping a school of piranhas for friends.")

They departed in silence, not pleased. Sarah put on her cap, took off her robe, gazed at the water with its shifting pattern of gold, remembered the slippery, glistening jeans. She did not swim.

Neither did she ask Tom's advice when she went to the hospital that night. The monitor had shown nothing that couldn't be handled by medication, but although his color was better Tom was in a state of deep depression. "Diet," he said. "Pills. The baby will think I'm its grandfather."

Sarah suspected that wasn't quite all. The other bed was flat and starchily immaculate: had that frail exhausted-looking old man really been judged fit to go home? It was a case of cheering up rather than confiding any worries of her own, and when Tom finally roused himself to say, "Did you swim?" Sarah answered without hesitation, "Yes. It was marvelous."

"How many lengths?"

It was a forty-foot pool. "Ten," said Sarah, and Tom looked pleased and then said anxiously, "Don't overdo it, now. What's the temperature?"

"Seventy-two," said Sarah, guessing, "and I won't overdo it, I promise."

The next day, after running the filter for four hours, she did swim, and the pool was all they had hoped for. She recovered the thermometer from the bottom and re-tied it, and it must have been injured because it read only sixty-eight degrees and the water was warmer than that. Polished green leaves turned gently above her; she moved through an ice-blue taffeta rustle. With a dim notion of undoing her lie to Tom she swam twenty lengths and then did some pleasurable dawdling. It was a surprise to realize that she had better make the most of this, because tomorrow—

They came in force, Louis and Marisol, the two older boys, and two girls. Although the girls didn't look over fifteen, one of them was cradling an infant of two or three months. Sarah's stomach muscles tightened involuntarily, because they had also brought beer and this was something she would have to put a stop to right away—Oh, God, if only Tom were home!

She went outside, her smile feeling varnished on, her heart thudding. She was completely taken aback when the girl without the baby said courteously, "Mrs. Birchall, I'm Karen Sales, and I think you're awfully kind to let us swim. Or are we interrupting? Say the word and we'll take right off."

The practiced air did not register at once, and Sarah heard herself answering that she could swim later. Before she could mention the beer, the girl went on in a confidential tone, "Would you mind a little music, if we kept it down? Tina"—she nodded at her encumbered friend—"has had sort of a rough time, and music soothes her."

Sarah swallowed. "Oh, is that her own baby?"

"Well, hers and Jimmy's," said the girl.

Jimmy, whom Sarah had thought to be about fourteen and could be sixteen at the most—thin, dark, stringy-muscled. She glanced about her, and there was a delicately nightmare quality in the sunlight; the baby, the beer being zipped open by people who, technically, were scarcely more than children. And none of them invited. She thought that no matter what Tom's condition was when she saw him this afternoon she would have to say, "What should I do?"

The instinctive answer wasn't necessarily the best. Order them off—and have slashed tires and broken windows? How could she even implement such an

order? The boys were as tall as she was and undoubtedly stronger; the girls, busily making themselves
comfortable, had an adamant air. Even a casual day-
by-day survey would have told them that she was
alone here although she had been careful not to tell
them so.

If she ordered them to go and they refused, or simply pretended not to hear, she would be infinitely
worse off than now.

Wait it out, she told herself, this one last time. Feeling, in her own backyard, as if she had invaded their
territory and was being driven off, Sarah went back
into the house.

Presently there was the sound of a car in the driveway. More beer arrived, this time in bottles, borne
by boys who appeared to be about eighteen. Hard-
rock music began to swell, not from a transistor but,
when Sarah went transfixedly to the back door, a
stereo hooked up to the outside light socket, from
which they had removed the bulb. The baby, presumably asleep, had been placed on a towel on the deck
under the full burning force of the sun.

Sarah was fiercely glad, because it took this to
strengthen her legs and give her no pause for further
thought. She ran outside, hearing a beer bottle shatter
on the way, catching no particular eye but calling
out imperatively, "Marisol, Louis—all of you! I'm
sorry, but we can't have this. Leave, please, this minute."

A tremble caught her, late; she tried to conceal it
by lifting her head militantly. A voice, she didn't

know whose, shouted above the blaring music, "That's right, her old man's coming home for a swim."

Laughter, and then: "Who's she?"

"Chick that owns the house, man. I vote we get out."

"Oh, right." Something thoughtful about it. "Don't want to bother the lady, it's her pool."

There was a scramble of tanned legs, and the afternoon had gone dangerously wrong: Louis and Marisol had pelted away without even taking their towels. Sarah couldn't identify the arm that pushed her—she hadn't even known that one of them was behind her. The water rushed up to meet her and then she was in the pool, clumsily, without a chance to dive, even her light clothing dragging at her. She kicked off her sandals at once, but shock and the naked fear she hadn't admitted to herself interfered with her breathing, and when she surfaced she was coughing and gasping.

And they were gazing down at her as if she were going to perform some interesting aquatic feat. Not children any more, but precocious young adults who had turned casually vicious at the end of a long hot summer because she, a newcomer at that, had something they did not. And now the power was reversed. Frank, or Jimmy, lifted the record player from the edge of the pool and poised it over his head. He said, "Gonna get a shock, Mrs. Birchall."

But that couldn't kill her—or could it? Sarah screamed, "Don't! I'm—" and found that even in this extremity she could not tell these savages that she was going to have a baby; it might act as a spur. From awe or a touch of fright, the girls had assumed expressions of—excitement?

Sarah swam toward the ladder, didn't dare grip the metal rails, swam away again. The record player seemed to blot out the sky. Then Karen who had spoken so politely had positioned herself at the pool steps. Spite hissed on the air like an invisible wind.

Sarah, who had swum twenty lengths without effort the day before, was already out of breath in this pinioned position—and nobody would come; nobody. They could play games with her as long as it entertained them, except that it wasn't a game any longer. Their control had left them the instant she hit the water.

In her terror her ears had begun to fill with a roaring—but it wasn't a distortion of her senses. Boy and record player were sent sprawling to the ground by the iron hand of huge, mustached Mr. Sandoval, who serviced the pool and carried fifty-pound bags of salt on one shoulder as though they were feathers.

The single roar—produced when he had been drawn to the pool by the sight of those intent and motionless backs—had been enough. Except for Sarah, Mr. Sandoval, and the abandoned record player, the back yard was empty.

Mr. Sandoval helped her out of the pool, keeping his look firmly at eye level because of her dripping, clinging dress. When he had asked her if she was all right, and she had nodded mutely because her mouth was trembling and she would cry if she tried to speak, he glanced down at the record player and said, "This yours? No?"—and gave it a demolishing kick.

He seemed to know intuitively that she had to be left alone for a few moments. He said cheerfully, "Better get on with my business here," and hefted the bag of salt he had dropped and vanished into the pump room with it.

Sarah stood motionless under the tree, gradually stopped shaking, then turned slowly to gaze at the pool. It was not contaminated *forever*, she thought fiercely; that would have been the ultimate triumph. They had gone, and she knew that with a witness, and such a witness as huge Mr. Sandoval, they would not come back.

She also knew that she would never tell Tom.

Mr. Sandoval backed his enormous frame out of the pump house, measured her, and judged her, by now, safe to address. "Who were they?" he asked curiously.

The leaves turned gently overhead. Had they swallowed those animal echoes forever? "I don't really know," said Sarah. "Just—kids."

A Beneficial Walk

By MARCH, two months into their regime of a daily constitutional in all weathers, the non-social Morrisroes had discovered themselves to be the apple of everyone's eye.

Was it because simple walking, as opposed to running or jogging, had become something of a lost art in the Southwest? Was it their ages, Blake's sixty and Lucy's fifty-two? Or, in an uneasy world, did such an activity speak of sensible discipline, marital accord, almost of a salute to the flag?

Whatever the reason, their heads-up, shoulders-back energy—they covered a mile and a half in a respectable twenty-seven minutes—came to be greeted by waves and friendly taps of the horn from the other regulars on their various routes, starting at eleven thirty: mailman, deputy sheriff on his patrol, school-bus driver, amiable strangers driving forth on punctual errands. It was as if, in undertaking the walks to give a definite shape to the day since Blake's retirement, the Morrisroes were bestowing a good upon the community.

"I believe we could run for office," said Lucy.

There was about them none of the subtle physical resemblance which sometimes creeps over the long-married. Blake, tall and spare, clipped as to features, had once, on a trip to California, been mistaken for David Niven. Small blue-eyed Lucy, delicate-skinned even in this climate, blonde hair now tinted fawn, could have slipped into any fashionable woman's club meeting without further credentials.

Although she looked as if she would be more at home among the teacups, it was she who poured the large sherries with which they rewarded themselves faithfully as soon as they were out of their gloves and coats. Next, she spent a few minutes writing busily in her journal.

It was a habit acquired years ago, and invaluable when it came to settling small debates as to what had happened when. At this time of day Lucy chronicled, among other things, meadowlarks and boat-tailed grackles, encounters with people, adventures with dogs. At first, because pedestrians were relatively unknown here and dogs responded accordingly, Blake had had to do a lot of stick-flourishing, but gradually their shapes and footsteps and voices grew to be known and accepted. There was tail-wagging, and, midway through their round-the-block walk, grave escort as far as the corner by a huge shaggy brown animal, undoubted king of his street.

Deputy Sheriff Richard "Dick" Tracy—his parents were responsible for his Christian name with its inevitable shortening and genes for his earnest jaw, but his outlandish and mirth-provoking wristwatch could be laid at his own door—Dick was ignorant of the journal's existence, but he saluted the Morrisroes almost daily. On an April morning of such blasting wind that along with a headscarf Lucy was wearing sunglasses as a protection against stinging sand and dust, he cruised after them as they re-entered their driveway at three minutes of twelve.

"Have to hand it to you folks, day like this," he said, shooting out his arm and grasping the top of the patrol car for full display of the watch which could do everything but play the piano. "Say, you didn't happen to notice anything funny going on at the Schuyler place yesterday, did you?"

The Schuyler domicile, situated on a winding stretch of road known locally and inaccurately as Millionaires' Row, was white, imposingly two-storied, and wrought-iron-balconied under its Spanish tile roof.

"They were having their rugs steam-cleaned," said Lucy with promptness. "At least that's what the van turning out—" She stopped short.

"Getting cleaned out, more likely," said Deputy Sheriff Tracy, pointing his jaw importantly. "Coin collection, most of it gold, and jewelry." He switched off his chattering radio and climbed out of the patrol car. "Got a minute?"

In the Morrisroes' living room, which had the warmth and slight shabbiness of well-rubbed velvet, he refused sherry and eyed their cigarettes as if he had discovered a pair of worms in a peach with a wholesome outer bloom. "You saw the van about when, would you say?"

"Eleven forty or so," said Blake, "because we go as far as the Arabian horse place just beyond there."

"Make?"

They couldn't help him with that, nor had they

seen the license plate, which they would not have
paid attention to in any case, because they were walking south and the van had turned north, but it had
been white with either very dark blue or black lettering, "Carpet Steam-Cleaning" on the side.

"We should have known right then, I suppose,"
said Lucy, casting a glance at Blake. "No company
name, no telephone number? Wait a second . . ."

She plucked her journal from the bookcase, turned
pages, read, presently reported with a shake of her
head, " 'Cleaning van at Schuylers!' Not much help,
but somehow you don't think of a thing like that going
on in broad daylight."

Deputy Tracy conceded reluctantly that the van
might have been legitimate, a one-man, door-to-door
operation, since the robbery could have taken place
at any time between eleven o'clock, when the Schuylers had departed for a week in Mexico, and nine this
morning, when Mr. Schuyler's sister had arrived from
Santa Fe to take charge during their absence. They
had relied on their German shepherd, and the boy
who came to feed it in mid-afternoon, for the interim.

"With a gold-coin collection?" said Lucy disbelievingly.

"Well, they have timed lights and they left their
other Cadillac pulled up in front, but you'd be surprised," Tracy told her absentmindedly. A smile was
beginning to steal over his face, firm and rosy although he wasn't far from retirement himself. "I guess
you folks are friends with every dog for miles around
by now."

Blake, who had lifted his glass, set it down with

sharpness. "I find that a very offensive remark, officer."

Tracy raised a placating palm. "Kidding, kidding."

"I don't know that you are," said Blake, coming
to his feet. "My wife and I explore the neighborhood
regularly, we are in a position to see people making
trip preparations, we are familiar with the local dogs.
Inspect the premises, if you will be so kind, for a
coin collection and jewelry."

"Mr. Morrisroe, Mrs. Morrisroe—"

"I mean it," said Blake between his teeth.

It wasn't a big house and it didn't take long. The
Morrisroes' daughter and only child, Maria, made pe-
riodic descents in her Triumph Spitfire from her new
job and apartment in Denver, collecting the belongings she had stored in the parental home for years,
so that the closet in the second bedroom was empty
and the bureau nearly so. That left only a bath and
a half—grimly, Blake removed the covers of the toilet
tanks—the dining room, larger bedroom, and kitchen.

Tracy's neck was scarlet by the time Blake had up-
ended Lucy's jewel box on the coverlet of the double
bed, yanked open every drawer, whipped the sliding
closet doors along their runners.

"Take your time, we'll finish our sherry if you don't
mind. Of course, you haven't looked up the chimney
and there are always my wife's flower borders, although I warn you that you'll never hear the end
of it if you harm her daffodils and hyacinths. And
how about the orchard? *There's* a hiding place for
you."

"Blake," said Lucy mildly, "don't needle this nice

man who is only doing the job you foisted on him."

"I thank you," said Tracy with heavy dignity, and at the door five minutes later, hand extended, "No hard feelings?"

"Would you expect them to be soft?" inquired Blake.

Tracy laughed appreciatively, as if a joke had been made, and reverted to officialdom with a glance at his watch. And some drastic error was showing up in one of its host of tiny windows, because he brought his wrist closer with wounded incredulity. Then, realizing himself to be in the presence of two suspiciously poker faces, he said stiffly, "Had no idea it was this late," and settled his cap squarely and departed.

Ten days later a second break-in took place a half mile from the Schuylers', and although here there was a methodical looping and festooning of toilet paper and most of a bottle of Scotch had been decanted on the living-room rug, the police were convinced that the same perpetrator, perhaps with a lookout, had simply added some embroidery with intent to confuse.

For one thing, each house was set well back on approximately two acres, with access from the broad bank of an irrigation ditch behind. For another, television sets and expensive hunting rifles had again been ignored in favor of jewelry, both men's and women's—a wafer-thin platinum pocket watch valued at $5,000 was among the spoils—and some antique silver.

As the robbery rate was very low in this generally well-protected area, an indignation meeting was held in the village hall. The Morrisroes attended, and spoke up in defense of the sheriff's department, which was being muttered at; they suggested that people who informed the newspapers when they were going to attend a black-tie dinner at the country club for patrons of the theater were asking for trouble unless they arranged for a house-sitter.

It was true, and it also followed that the woman in question would wear her second-best jewelry to the dinner; she would save the real dazzle for the next evening, the opening night of the new season.

Officer Tracy did not pay a second call on the Morrisroes in the hope of any chance witnessing because the robbery had taken place between six thirty and midnight. Even apart from that, a downpour which was the fringe of a late-spring blizzard in Colorado, incidentally keeping Maria from a scheduled visit home, would have daunted the bravest walkers.

Nor was the rain the help it should have been, softening the sandy bank for footprints or other tracks. The new and dinner-partying victims, having dropped earrings and necklace and bracelet and cufflinks sleepily into a drawer of the dressing table in their bath, did not discover their loss until mid-morning. By that time early Saturday riders had been out, leaving the bank a churned welter of hoofmarks.

The storm system passed, and Blake and Lucy resumed their brisk perambulations. It only registered on the third day that they had not been lightly honked at by the familiar figure in the police cruiser. A sensible juggling of timetables, because after a period of months a predictable patrol lost a good part of its

usefulness? Or re-assignment of Officer Tracy as a
mark of official displeasure? The Morrisroes, who had
attended the indignation meeting largely in his defense—they considered him an excellent man for the
job—sincerely hoped not.

The steam-cleaning van they had described as leaving the first scene was unfindable in spite of newspaper and television publicity. In an age of spray paint
it wasn't surprising. For that matter, everyone said
wisely, the lettering could have been decals.

On Thursday night Maria called from Denver to
say that she would be driving down for the weekend.
Late on Friday afternoon, with her bedroom readied
and a celebratory bottle of Piper-Heidseick chilling,
Blake and Lucy sauntered out to the orchard so mockingly put forward to Officer Tracy.

There, the deep tangle of grass around one particular apple tree was just that. No dark-green vinyl trash
bag remained, its contents not fertilizer or garden
waste but a glowing, sparkling, shimmering hoard.
The sole trace of vanished treasure was a rounded
oblong of yellowing stems, their tops brushed so
neatly upright that from a window view the Morrisroe secret was intact.

It was now cruelly clear where the deputy sheriff
had been when they missed him on their recent walks:
coming relentlessly back once he was sure they were
well away from the house, aware, as apparently dense
people can be, that he had been baited and laughed
at. He wouldn't have dug up Lucy's flower borders,
leaving disturbed earth behind him, but the mention

of the orchard had set off a slow and cumbrous train of thought.

The house itself was one thing; the outdoors another. In the unlikely event of premature discovery the Morrisroes could say in amazement that someone local had obviously taken note of their walking schedule and seized upon their orchard with its long grass as a safe cache until disposition could be made of the diamonds and emeralds and sapphires, the platinum and coin collection and antique silver.

The Morrisroes had been augmenting their income in various ways for years, Blake so deft with his fingers that few locks resisted him and Lucy listening quickwittedly to other women when she had her hair tinted. The confidences to be heard were astonishing, such as the date and length of the Schuylers' trip to Mexico.

That foray had been a trifle dangerous, even though the German shepherd had been almost pathetically glad to see them, but well worth it. All at once, however, there was a new complexion on things.

What if the police should find out that these orchard-owners had been interrogated and reluctantly let go for lack of proof in Westport, Connecticut, in Larchmont, New York, in Tucson, Arizona? Those had been peccadillos compared to the confiscated haul.

Blake and Lucy rushed into the house and switched on the local news. Not a word was said about approximately $175,000 in missing valuables.

There couldn't be two interpretations of that. Tracy, of custom called Dick, with his comic-strip jaw and his ludicrous watch, would plod into retirement with their riskily garnered gains. And there wasn't a single thing the Morrisroes could do about it.

If there had been no storm the previous weekend, if Maria had been able to make her intended visit . . . but Maria, beguilingly pony-tailed and looking much younger than her actual twenty-eight, would now make the run from Denver for nothing. Her reliable contact in California would rub his anticipatory palms in vain, because this particular scoop was going to come up empty.

When the first shock wave had passed, the Morrisroes contemplated each other with resignation. At least, they reminded themselves over a powerful martini, they had their health.

A small silence fell, while Lucy gazed out at tearing wind and rolling tumbleweeds. "Palm Springs sounds nice," she said presently. "But wouldn't it be a trifle hot for walking?"

Snowball

THE COTTAGE had had a gingerbread look in the last of the afternoon light: snow in a steep frosting on its tilted roof, frost rimming its small window-panes. I remember now that we knocked, both secretly knowing the absurdity of it, and that walking into that living room was as shocking as opening a Christmas card to find an obscene verse inside.

It wasn't only the blood on the floorboards, or the brass gleam of the poker standing primly at attention on the hearth. Part of it was the table set for tea at the shadowy end of the room—napkins folded, teapot in a quilted cosy, crusts of bread in a savage litter on the braided rug. And on the window sill in the alcove, like a travesty of domestic comfort, the cat, Snowball.

Beside me, Madden called in his high irritable voice, "Charles?" and in the same split second I shouted, "Anne?"

That was symbolic. Both of us knew that only one of the Jethros could possibly answer, the one who had killed the other.

It's hard to explain about the Jethros. Even Madden, who had been Charles Jethro's literary agent for eighteen years, confessed himself baffled. Maybe that was because each of them had two separate personalities,

which made a total of four people living together for
twenty years.

You may have read some of Jethro's essays, or attended one of the gatherings at which he was in constant demand as a speaker. He was a big man, about
fifty, and handsome in a craggy disarming way. He
was sensitive about his failing eyesight and never
wore his thick glasses in public, but somehow he contrived a keen and twinkling air when he spoke at
what must have been an indistinguishable blur. He
had made two successful departures into the field of
verse. *Broiled Offerings*, a sizzling parody of the obscu-
rist school of poetry, was followed by *Puzzles in Smoke*,
which the enlightened public bought with great antic-
ipation and the critics circled as warily as a strange
dog, because it might or might not be another parody.

That was the Charles Jethro who sparkled at select
cocktail parties and wrote witty inscriptions in his
books for favored friends. You had to have known
him a long time to be even acquainted with the brutal,
vindictive, incredibly foul-tempered man who shared
the same skin.

His wife Anne, who was perhaps five years younger
than he, was his right hand, his amanuensis, his quietly unerring critic. Someone had been unkind
enough to call her his seeing-eye bitch; I often wondered if Jethro himself had thought that up. She was
one of those willfully neglected-looking women, with
tweeds that never quite fitted and tan hair strained
back into a knot. Somewhere in her family there had
been an admixture of some surprising blood; her
mouth was heavy and her eyes as unfathomable as

black bean soup. She did Jethro's typing—he would trust it to no one else—and kept him to deadlines and defended him from nuisances like a tigress when he was working.

But the steadiness and the constancy had its other side. No one could bear a grudge as implacably as Anne Jethro, or seethe as long, with the lid on tight, like some dangerous stew. When her hand was forced there was usually a hatpin inside—like the time when Jethro had insisted on her entertaining a trio of visiting Englishwomen at tea, and she had docilely cut watercress sandwiches and plum cake. Opened up, the dainty little napkins revealed, in indelible ink, an unrepeatable phrase about Jethro.

"Charles?" called Madden again from the foot of the stairs, and turned back to me. He said, as though he could hold something at bay by his disapproval, "I don't like this at all, I believe I'll have a look upstairs. I wish that damned cat wouldn't sit there like that."

The cat, Snowball, was a pledge of Jethro's malice towards his wife just as certainly as a diamond pin was a pledge of another man's affection. Anne hated and feared cats with the same violent reaction women usually reserve for rats, and I had seen her driven from the room more than once by this one. Jethro had taken it in as a stray, and named it sardonically— if he had adopted a dog he would have insisted on calling it Fido—and while he caviled at Anne's housekeeping expenditures he fed it on salmon and sardines. He took a perverse delight in its greed and selfishness and haughty tail-switchings, for the simple reason that the cat repelled and frightened his wife.

Because the Jethros hated each other.

Why did they stay together? Their few close friends advanced various theories. They were used to each other, they were actually stimulated by their weird domestic battles, Charles needed Anne emotionally and Anne was financially dependent on Charles—and so forth.

Madden was much too clever to say anything that might be quoted behind his back, but I had always thought it was *because* at bottom they hated each other, and were bound in a mutual pact of revenge. Charles twisted Anne's wrist in one of his ungovernable tempers, and Anne—silent, implacable—hid his glasses for a week while he begged piteously for them. Or Charles hid his glasses himself as an excuse for not making out a cheque for Anne's housekeeping money, and Anne marched off to the nearest pawnshop with his mother's heirloom silver.

People who knew them laughed over these colorful irregularities—"Did you know Jethro hit Anne with one of those baked-bean casseroles?" "No, really? I thought she smashed them all the night those people from Boston came to dinner"—and any uneasiness they felt was slight. Charles could somehow emerge from one of these sessions at his blandest and wittiest, and Anne, sometimes nursing a wrist or a shin, would be calm and helpful with autograph seekers.

But then they had moved to Byfield, the two of them—or the four of them?—into the snows and the

silences and the confines of a cottage deep in the country, on the estate of a friend of Jethro's. The move
had been partly Madden's idea, to coax out an evalua-
tion of Joyce: Jethro on Joyce, he said in an authorita-
tive squeak, would set the literary world by the ears.

But—the snows, the silence, the very aloneness. No
friends dropping in, no convivial engagements outside
to break into that tiny, too closely bound world. Anne
and Jethro both had the profoundest respect for Jethro's ability, but that wasn't enough. There was nothing to stimulate Jethro into being bland and witty,
or Anne into shelving her grudges; nothing to check
the outbreak of rage, and everything to feed it. I had
visited them once for an hour or two on the way
down from Boston, and I went away feeling as though
I had gotten out of a lion's cage. Bare trees and frozen
shrubs in burlap and the whistling bitter wind aren't
for people who hate each other, with no one to see
what they do about it. It was as if something had
begun to snowball.

The cat—had Jethro named her more originally
than he thought?—watched me complacently as I
started out of the living room. Upstairs, Madden was
clumping about with the heavy tread common to
small men who want to make their weight felt. I
walked into the tiny old-fashioned kitchen, but there
was nothing there to tell me anything, even if the
dusk hadn't begun to close in. The surfaces were bare,
the wooden cabinets closed and blank; the black stove
Anne had joked about was cold when I touched it.
That would make it—how long since Anne had

killed Charles, or Charles had killed Anne?

Madden came downstairs again, tiptoeing solemnly. In spite of his superbly cut cashmere suit and his glowing foulard tie he looked old and cold and worried; for all his petulant squeakings and his ruthless determination to get a book out of his client, he had been fond of Jethro—and Jethro guilty of murder would be in almost as bad a pickle as Jethro dead. He said irritably, "Turn on a light, will you? I suppose we'll have to call the police."

"You'll have to call very loudly then," I said, as jumpy as he was. "The lights are out and so is the phone. All this white stuff is a blizzard, Madden. They get them in the country. We'll have to drive into the village."

"You go," said Madden, making a large gesture for so small a man. "There are candles somewhere, I suppose, and I'll know where to look for his notes and manuscript and things. My God, we don't want the manuscript impounded. Poor Charles."

"Or poor Anne," I said.

The car wouldn't start. I suppose cars never do under such circumstances, although this wasn't entirely coincidental; Madden, whose car we had driven up from New York in, had in his agitation left the ignition on and the battery was dead.

I scuffled back to the cottage in almost complete darkness, trying to keep to the track we had trampled through the snow when we first arrived. Somewhere under the unmarred surface on either side there had to be other footprints—Jethro's, plungingly deep as he carried Anne's body, or Anne's as she had dragged

Jethro's—but snow couldn't be peeled back in layers like blankets.

Madden had found candles when I returned, and set them up on the neat, ghastly tea table. The flickering light reached out to the bloodstains, turning them black and caught a knowing wink from the poker. I told him about the car and he said absently, "Oh," and then in a queer voice, "The manuscript is gone, and all his notes. Eight months' work. She might at least," he said bitterly, "have left us that."

"Jethro may have taken them himself, as—insurance. Anne would have killed the cat," I said. "Jethro wouldn't have."

Snowball watched us noncommittally.

Madden wet his lips. "Anne was probably afraid to kill it, afraid it might spring at her."

"If she killed Jethro she would have killed the cat. As," I said uncomfortably, "part of Jethro. If you follow that."

"I can't say that I do, quite," said Madden snappishly. "The thing is—when?"

What he meant was, how far had one of them gotten with the Joyce manuscript and the notes with which to finish it? Madden had wired Jethro two days ago about an offer from *Harper's* for a series of essays on modern poetry; it was the kind of thing that Jethro would have jumped at, and when a further telephone call—that must have been before the wires went down—produced no response, Madden had gotten worried enough to call me and propose a trip to Byfield.

I suppose an expert could have told from the appearance of the bloodstains how old they were; we were only certain of what they had to mean. But the cat hadn't been ravenous enough to finish the crusts of bread on the floor beneath the tea table, or thirsty enough to overturn the cream jug, so that it must have been fed the day before. Unless—

"You're sure," I said to Madden over a brief stomach-turning, "that there's *nothing* upstairs?"

"I don't know what you mean by nothing," began Madden crossly, engrossed in his own problems, and looked at Snowball, washing her whiskers with a satisfied air, and turned pale. "My God, how can you even—no, of course not."

So that placed the time of death—Anne's, or Jethro's—at just before tea time yesterday. With the snow falling, it would have been dark then, and the electricity had been off. And still there had been blood spilled, the poker wiped and put back—all in the dark?

The candles Madden had found in a drawer were new, just now beginning to form shaky threads of wax. There were no kerosene lamps in the house. I stood up, following the vaguest of thoughts, and Snowball moved too.

Madden recoiled at the sudden soft thump. The cat sniffed at a crust and spurned it, and then stalked in a horribly intent way across the floor towards the bloodstains. When she was nearly there she turned around and began briskly to sharpen her claws on one of the small braided rugs with which the living room was furnished.

And the rugs slid. As Snowball sharpened away,

the bloodstains disappeared under the twisting pattern. An instant later I noticed the candles in the sconce on the inside living room wall, pale yellow in a black iron holder, and burned almost halfway down.

Those candles, then, had provided the light for murder. With the rug in place over the stains, anyone entering the cottage as a matter of neighborly concern might think that the Jethros had merely gone away for a few days.

Except for the cat. For Anne, it must have been a symbol of hatred. Jethro, on the other hand, would have left it food and water enough to last it until he could come back—or would he, once it had served its purpose?

I heard Madden saying with the waspishness of deep worry, "Well, what is it?" but I went on staring at the right-hand candle. They both leaned a little out from the wall, but the frozen waterfall of wax on that one was *facing* the wall. So it had been taken out of the sconce.

We stayed in the cottage that night, partly because the only alternative was a four-mile walk through the freezing dark, mostly because the place held a curiously pending air. Possibly that was Snowball, back on the window sill, staring expectantly out at the night.

Madden had a flask in his luggage and we shared a couple of moody drinks. With the first shock gone the Jethros became again not killer and victim, but friends of long years' standing. Madden's concern was largely for Charles; I kept remembering what intelligent good company Anne could be when she wasn't simmering.

The cottage was bitterly cold, but by mutual consent we kept away from the hearth and the poker. In the kitchen we found more candles, and in the black depths of the refrigerator the remains of a ham. The half-loaf of bread was faintly stale but we were both hungry; Madden, a dedicated gourmet, fell upon his sandwich as though it had been snails in his favorite sauce.

Snowball miaowed angrily in the doorway, and although I had seen Madden gazing speculatively at a can of sardines I put them in a saucer on the floor. When the cat had eaten and retired a short way to wash her face I said, "I suppose we'd better let her out."

"I wouldn't do that," said Madden. He didn't like cats but he had a semi-superstitious respect for them. "I think we ought to be able to see where she goes when she does go out."

There was something frightful in the suggestion of the cat sniffing her way daintily to the corpse, and although it was plain that Madden didn't like it either he said stubbornly, "Didn't Charles have a run for her when they first moved out here?"

There was a short wire-enclosed run behind the cottage; I remembered, on an earlier visit, seeing Snowball batting at the fluffy white flowers on a bush that grew beside it. I opened the kitchen door and ushered her out, and before the wind blew the candle out I saw her vault lightly into the enclosure. She didn't care for the cold or the snow, and she scratched at the door before Madden had finished his second sandwich.

After that there was nothing to do but go to sleep. It didn't occur to either of us to occupy the Jethros' beds. We retired to chairs, covered ourselves with our overcoats, and smoked a final cigarette.

"You know," said Madden suddenly, in the slightly lowered tone we had both used unconsciously ever since entering the cottage, "there wasn't much daylight left to look around in. Maybe there's a note."

I couldn't help but stare. "Out burying body, back soon?"

"It was just a thought," said Madden, looking offended, and blew out the candle.

But there was, after all, something to the suggestion. If the braided rug had been pulled over the bloodstains and the poker and the candle replaced in order to conceal the crime from a casual eye, mightn't there be a note?

Anne was meticulous over details; she would never have put the candle into its holder backwards, so that the flow of wax ran the wrong way. *But nearsighted Charles wouldn't have noticed the way.* Or had Anne thought of that, and acted accordingly?

And was that why Snowball was alive?

It occurred to me on the edge of sleep that, barring the fingerprints which the merest child knew enough not to leave around, it was going to take a little while, even for the police to figure out which of the Jethros was dead and which to spread a dragnet for. They were the same blood type; that had come out years ago when Charles needed a transfusion after a severe operation. Unless there were hairs on the poker, long tan ones, or grey-tipped black—

I closed my eyes in the darkness, trying to wipe out the vision that summoned up, and when I opened them the room was blue with early daylight.

There was no note; Madden looked for one while I made instant coffee with cold water, achieving an indescribable effect. We were both chilled and stiff and edgy, and there was a short sharp discussion over which of us would walk into the village to get the police. Madden won, or lost, whichever way you look at it, and he had his hand on the doorknob when we suddenly stared at each other, struck by one of those weird communications of thought.

I said, "Had you better check the nearest hospital first?"

"My God . . . of course. They got cabin fever, and she hit him—"

"Or he hit her—"

"—and realized that this time it had gone too far," interrupted Madden, waving an impatient hand, "and called a doctor and went off to the hospital. It's as simple as that. What idiots we've been, they've been doing this for years on a minor scale. Maybe it's a good thing, teach them both a lesson. I suppose it's all over the front page of the local paper, but that can't be helped. Well, I'm off, I'll be back as soon as I can."

All this didn't explain the missing manuscript, or the fact that the poker and the candle had been put back so tidily, but it did clear up the pending atmosphere, the presence of the cat and, most important of all, the disappearance of *both* the Jethros. Charles could have carried Anne's body, and Anne could have dragged his, but what to do with it then?

It would have been impossible to dig a grave in that frozen ground even if there had been tools to work with, and the property wasn't furnished with any convenient wells or ravines, or even woods, at any handy distance. It was flat and park-like, with a tree here and there and a scattering of winterized shrubs. There were no masses of rhododendrons or pines to offer any kind of concealment.

An embargo had been lifted, and I let Snowball out and followed her into the brilliant morning. Maybe Madden was right and this would be a lesson to the Jethros, like delirium tremens to a drinker or an accident to a careless driver. It should certainly teach them to stick to bean casseroles instead of pokers.

Snowball jumped up on the kitchen steps and began a protracted bath; she paused briefly to measure a distant sparrow and then went back to her plumy tail. Beyond her was the wire run, the wrapped bush that bore white flowers in the spring, and a lot of greyish twiggy growth. Bayberry? I knew that it grew around here; Anne was fond of it.

It wasn't bayberry, and it wasn't growing. It looked at first like a tree bough blown down by the wind, but it wasn't that either because the end had been sawed cleanly through.

I suppose I knew what it was then, and why the cat had been allowed to live. The burlap was knotted firmly around the base of the bush when I dug down through the snow, and in the end I had to go back into the cottage for a knife. For me, the pending air was gone, the savage message delivered.

The burlap kept its shape grotesquely in the icy air when I lifted it off. It was the arched and appalling shape of Charles Jethro, frozen wrists tied to frozen ankles, both lashed securely to the base of the bush that had borne the fat white flowers. The snowball bush.